The Rescue of
the Forgotten Children

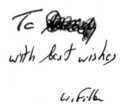

To ~~Danny~~
with best wishes

W. Fisher

Biddles

Biddles Books Limited
Castle House
East Winch Road
Blackborough End
King's Lynn
Norfolk PE32 1SF

Biddles

email: enquiries@biddles.co.uk
Web: www.biddles.co.uk

Cover Design and Illustration: Cong Nguyen

ISBN: 978-1-915292-26-1

British Library Cataloguing in Publication Data.
A catalogue record for this book is
available from the British Library.

Printed and bounded by Biddles Books Ltd, Norfolk, PE32 1SF.

I dedicate this book to Sir Nicholas Winton, a remarkable man, who with the help of Doreen Warriner and other courageous souls, saved over 669 children, before Hitler invaded Poland on September 1, 1939.

The characters in this novella apart from Nicholas Winton, his mother and Doreen Warriner bear no relation to any living person. All names of children, their parents, Nazi Party members, SS officers are fictional and places and positions are the products of the author's imagination or used fictitiously. In writing this book, I based my story on publicly available facts to loosely recreate the events which took place in Prague, six months before the start of the Second World War.

Chapter 1. An Unexpected Phone Call

The late afternoon dust light motes, scintillated the senses as the men shimmied their way around and about the London sports hall. Hands held their metal fencing epees and moved confidently as white dresses floated back and forth in the dance of retreating and lunging forward to attack. Nicholas Winton, in his late twenties, moved intently and with deadly precision, hitting the torso of his opponent. He riposted and attacked. Suddenly, the opponent parried back and soon both epees were lunging and bouncing back and forth, over and over again. After a few minutes, the erratic movement of feet ceased.

Nicholas took off his mask and faced Bob.

"Well played, Bob," Nicholas said.

"Brilliant game," said Bob. "Revenge next time?"

"Sure, Bob."

"Are you ready for your holiday, old chum?" asked Bob.

"I haven't even packed yet."

It was an early evening as Nicholas walked down the well—established area in London. He glanced at the posh style buildings, noticeable as self—assured and impeccably dressed in an elegant suit. A strong wind blew the large raindrops into his face, but nothing could perturb him and he smiled broadly. He quickened his pace up to his apartment.

As he entered, he took off his grey overcoat and put a bag with his fencing equipment aside.

"Hello, Ma," he shouted from the foyer.

"How was fencing?" asked Barbara.

"It was good, Ma. Bob led me a merry chase."

Nicholas entered the kitchen, pleasantly decorated and filled with warm colours. A blue vase on top of a table added a pleasant feel to the place and showed his Ma's touch.

"Are you excited about your holiday?" she asked.

Smiling, Nicholas turned to her. "I can't wait."

"Don't forget to write a letter when you arrive, though."

"I will do, Ma," Nicholas answered as he leaned in to hug her.

"This is the first time I will be travelling to Switzerland; it's going to be quite an adventure. I am looking forward to all the skiing and the cuisine. Martin has been travelling for quite a bit, and he knows all the good spots on and off the slopes."

"How is Martin doing in Czechoslovakia?"

"Busy Ma. He is embroiled in the volunteering job he applied for in Prague," he replied.

"I hope he is happy there…such a dear boy, with a good heart," she said.

The ringing of the telephone interrupted their conversation.

Nicholas went into the hallway and the sound of his shoes echoed on the dark, wooden floorboard. He picked up the phone and as he looked down at the pattern on the decent size Persian carpet, he answered.

"Hello…Who is it? Martin?! I can hardly hear you, pal. Very well, I understand. Yes, Martin, I am listening. A New Year celebration in Prague. Let's do it. Sure, Martin. Speak to you soon."

Nicholas hung up the receiver and returned to his mother.

"Who was it?

"Martin."

"Martin? Well, what do you know! We were just discussing him now?" she said.

"The ski trip is off, but he wants me to join him in Prague to celebrate the New Year. He said something came up, and he wants to show me some places over there.

"The idea of welcoming the New Year in Prague could be a good idea."

"The idea appeals to me, Ma. There won't be any skiing, but the food is equally good," he said happily.

Nicholas turned around and headed up to start packing, whistling a dingle as he went along.

Chapter 2. New Year's Eve in Prague

The next evening Nicholas found himself sitting in an old vintage cab, rushing along the streets of Prague, the capital of Czechoslovakia, as the clocks in the city struck seven. In the ensuing dusk, the temperatures were suddenly dropping, with a spell of rain that was falling like a curtain, all over the city. Nicholas beamed with wonder, as he watched the busy traffic whizzing past his cab window. Everywhere he looked there were buses and cars, with countless people crowding the pavement, even in the discouraging weather. His young face glowed with excitement, as he fixed his gaze upon all the architectural wonders, he was passing by.

Suddenly, the exhilaration of the evening intensified as the cab stopped outside a luxurious hotel. In front of him was the Grand Hotel Šroubek, a magnificent building set in a square, in keeping with its splendid façade and crowned with gilded nymphs. The building was characterized by tall, impressive windows and ornate balconies. Across from it was the gleaming fourteenth—century Orloj Astronomical clock, displaying various astronomical dials and statues of the different Catholic saints, as they stood on either side of the clock.

As the rain patterned against the concrete, it flooded the street and washed clean every crack and crevice.

Nicholas cautiously exited the cab and quickly headed towards the hotel.

The door with the brass frame, swung open as Nicholas drew closer and as he entered, he was astounded by the hotel's exquisite, baroque interior. He walked across the tiled flooring and headed for the Reception Desk.

Hotel guests were milling around the foyer, anticipating the celebration of the New Year festivities. Men wearing elegant tuxedos were walking around with women that were resplendently decked out in the most exquisite gowns and jewels. Exotic perfumes were wafting here and there. The ebb and flow of animated voices could be heard resounding from every corner of the foyer, electrifying the enlivened atmosphere.

Suddenly a smartly, dressed man in his early thirties, emerged from the crowd. Enthusiastic and friendly as usual, he approached Nicholas with a beaming smile. As he came closer, he grabbed Nicholas in a bear hug, slapping him on the back.

"Welcome to Prague, old friend," said Martin. "Thank you for accepting my invitation and apologies for ruining your skiing holiday."

"Don't worry about that. There's always next year and I will make sure you make this up to me…old friend," Nicholas retorted with a twinkle in his eye.

"I'm very grateful you're here. I want to show you why my work here is very important."

They step into a spacious banquet hall, filled with at least two dozen round, beige, stone and marble tables.

More guests and visitors entered the exclusive hall, which was lit by opulent chandeliers. The guests were almost giddy with anticipation, exhilarated at the evening that lay ahead and the prospect of a new year, with new hope.

On the stage, a swing band was playing all the ragtime favourites, to the delight of the dancing couples on the dance floor. It was a feast for the eyes, with all the colours and textures swishing by. The tempo changed and the band began to play an old Czech jazz song from the mid—thirties.

"What a lively place," exclaimed Nicholas.

"Shall we join the banquet? It's almost midnight!" asked Martin.

"After you," replied Nicholas.

When Nicholas finally caught up with Martin, he was making his way over to the stage, where he spotted a friend standing. Martin waved to the well—dressed, good—looking man, who was sipping a drink from a tumbler glass. He was talking to a boisterous woman, standing a few feet away, as she swayed to the rhythm of the trombone's soulful soliloquy.

"Tim!" shouted Martin.

Tim spotted Martin shuffling over to him.

"How are you, Tim? I didn't know you were coming," said Martin.

"I needed a moment of normalcy…," said Tim.

"What's wrong?"

"It has been a hard year," said Tim, as he downed half of his drink.

"I am sorry to hear that."

"I brought two refugee boys back. I've placed them at a local school," explained Tim.

Martin turned to Tim. "Tim, this is my friend, Nicholas."

"Pleasure to meet you," says Nicholas.

"How do you do?" asked Tim.

"You're keeping yourself busy?" asked Martin.

"My mother wants to rescue a third child. The situation isn't pleasant. The poor children…," said Tim.

He turned to Nicholas. "You must do well, financially."

Nicholas appeared to be taken aback.

Martin gritted his teeth as his cheeks reddened.

"Tim, come on…".

"You look like a wealthy man. Maybe you could find a home for a child in England. There are so many of them out there," said Tim.

"I am not sure if that's something I could help with," Nicholas responded.

"I'm sure you could."

Nicholas looked at Martin, squirming under his scrutiny.

"Is this why you invited me here?"

"Nicholas…it's important to help the children…I wanted you to see for yourself."

A spotlight sliced through the gathered crowd. Everybody stopped dancing, as a loud cheer resounded throughout. On stage, the band stopped playing. An imposing maître d' in an elegant tuxedo grabbed the microphone.

"Ladies and gentlemen, quiet, please! The count-down is about to begin…ten, nine, eight, seven, six, five, four, three, two, and one! Happy New Year!" the maître d'yelled exuberantly, with joy beaming on his face.

"Happy New Year! Happy New Year!" could be heard from all around, as the guests shouted out their exhilaration.

A deluge of confetti showered the guests and embraces and kisses were dealt out by everyone. More champagne bottles could be heard popping all over the banquet hall and the sweet smell of the champagne wafted through the room.

"Cheers! Happy New Year!" said Martin, lifting a champagne glass.

"Happy New Year to all of you!" Tim piped up, lifting his tumbler.

Nicholas looked at the ground, disheartened at his friend's duplicity, but also at the same time understanding his motive. He looked up and then raised his tulip—shaped champagne glass.

"All the best for the year ahead!"

On stage, the band struck up a lively song.

The guests applauded and resume dancing, with an extra jaunt in their steps.

Nicholas sighed and touched his forehead, thoroughly deflated with the thought of the children and the desperation in Tim's eyes.

"Is everything all right?" asked Martin.

"I… I think I just need some rest if you don't mind. Good night, gentlemen," said Nicholas.

As he walked away, Martin tentatively asked, "Do you still want to visit those children?"

Nicholas turned around.

"You should, Nicholas," said Martin.

"Fine…let's do it tomorrow," and with that, he left, not realising that he was leaving his innocence and carefree life, behind him in the banquet hall.

Chapter 3. Visiting the Outskirts of Prague

It's was still early, with dawn barely peeking on the first day of a brand New Year, as a car pulled up on the outskirts of Prague. As the first light of the day broke through and dissolved the dark mist in the air, a district characterized by slums, showed its discouraged façade. Martin and Nicholas stepped out of the car as Doreen, bursting with energy, approached them. She wasn't knockout gorgeous, by something in her, kept drawing an eye and she was passionate about constantly seeking to promote human welfare.

Martin turned to Doreen.

"This is my friend, Nicholas."

"Delighted to meet you," said Doreen.

"Likewise."

They walked into the camp, the crisp air and iced ground crackling under their feet. The place was hell on earth, squalid and overcrowded, with smashed houses and shacks in shades of greyish, dirty brown, and piles of detritus everywhere. Stray dogs scurried around and enormous rats moved hurriedly, scurrying for food.

Suddenly, the first tendrils of the light seemed to reach into the darkness before Nicholas and rip open the ugly truth. Nicholas took it all in…desperate families with bone—thin and barefoot children. All of them dressed in threadbare, discoloured rags, all shivering uncontrollably in the cold.

"How long have you been doing this?" asked Nicholas.

"Nearly two months now," said Doreen softly.

Shocked, Nicholas spotted a bare—chested, raw—boned man struggling to get to his feet. He approached him and helped him to get back on his feet. He turned to Doreen, who watched him with pity, as his innocence was being stripped bare.

"My goodness, the conditions are inhuman," Nicholas whispered.

"I am sure Martin has already told you, we have British activists in Czechoslovakia."

"He has," said Nicholas, shocked, confused and ashamed.

"My role here is to help refugees escape to England, especially the ones on Hitler's blacklist," Doreen stated.

"Who are these people?" Nicholas asked, intrigued.

"Hitler's political enemies, leaders of the Sudeten Social Democratic Party and their children."

"Children, too?"

"There is no organisation set up yet to help them. Four children died last week. We desperately need help," she explained.

Nicholas gazed at four, famished—looking children, who stared at him with fear in their eyes. Their fear burned into his soul.

"Things can't go on like this. Those children are hungry and they cannot be safe here."

"You are right of course; all you say is true. They are all in danger and we simply don't have human resources or means to help them all," said Doreen, as she looked over the settlement, sighing sadly.

"I don't understand. Surely, we must be able to do something," said Nicholas.

"Unfortunately, there is no country that will take Hitler's enemies. There's not much we can do for the parents. The only solution is to evacuate the children."

Nicholas thought hard, his face reflective of deter-mination.

"Can you help, please?" asked Martin.

"I am not sure how I might help all these families," said Nicholas.

"Hitler's already taken control of the Sudetenland and most of Europe," said Doreen. "His plan is clearly to occupy the whole of Czechoslovakia. Things will turn nasty, as early as, six months from now. It will be tragic for every child left behind to die, don't you agree?"

She stared hard at Nicholas. He looked at the fire in her eyes, ill—at—ease with the prospect.

"Excuse me for a moment," she said.

She walked over to Dobromira Sarenka, mid—forties and malnourished. Dobromira coughed and sneezed. Her children Paulina, six years old and Pavel, eight years old, also suffered from ill—health. Pavel, racked by a nasty cough, sneezed into his shirt, trying to catch droplets on his elbow.

Nicholas approached Paulina and Pavel. He took a half—crown coin out. The children look at the coin, puzzled.

"That's English money," said Nicholas.

Dobromira approached Nicholas. "Will you find a home for my child?"

Nicholas, speechless, doesn't know what to say.

"Please, take care of my children. I want you to take them with you. I trust you. You are a good man," said Dobromira.

"I am not sure I can."

"Take them with you. I trust you. I want to know if they are in good hands. She could be your daughter. Listen to her sing. Paulina, Paulina…" repeated Dobromira.

Paulina looked up at her mother, her eyes almost shut by conjunctivitis. She scraped the thick pus off them.

Dobromira spoke to Paulina in Czech. "Let the nice Englishman hear your voice."

Paulina cleared her throat and sang in a weak voice. The lack of breath and weak supporting muscles overrode her desire and though she was desperate to continue, she couldn't.

Moved, Nicholas reached out and stroked her head. "Thank you, my child."

Dobromira looked straight into Nicholas's eyes. "She can cook for you, makes the best stew. I can assure you she can do a lot of things. She will be a good girl for you. When you will have a tough day, she will cook for you."

She wept uncontrollably. Tears welled up in Paulina's eyes and tears streamed down Pavel's face, as he held out his arms to Nicholas.

"I can't. I travel a lot; however, I can try to find a home for them. I can't guarantee anything though. If I find a place for them, I can't promise you would ever see them again," said Nicholas.

"Please. We have nowhere else to go," said Dobromira, as she shed more tears.

Nicholas turned to Martin. "There must be something we can do. Maybe I can at least try to save a few of the children."

Martin smiled broadly. Doreen had the sheen of unshed tears in her eyes and although she tried hard to contain her emotion, her relief was almost tangible.

"Anything would be helpful. Anything," said Doreen, as she wiped at her eyes.

Nicholas's mind was already racing ahead, the wheels turning fast as he contemplated plan after plan.

He nodded at Doreen. "I can't promise anything though."

Chapter 4. Disturbing Morning

The clock had barely struck six in the morning, on Nicholas's third day in Prague. A soft knock sounded on his hotel room's wooden, panelled door…and again. then again, with more urgency. The loud knock echoed, as Nicholas dried his face and hurried out to see what the clamour was all about. Barely awake, he opened the door.

Berta Cerny, in her thirties, unkept and malnourished, stood before him, wringing her hands.

"How can I help you?" asked Nicholas, surprised.

"Please…please, help my child," said Mrs Cerny.

Nicholas reeled with shock. This was not something he was expecting.

"How did you get past security?" asked Nicholas.

"My child…very sick. You must help!" replied Mrs Cerny, in tears.

"Please, wait for me downstairs," said Nicholas.

"No, no."

"I'll be right down, madam. I promise," said Nicholas.

"Thank you, thank you, sir."

Nicholas shut the door and rushed to get dressed.

Later in the hotel lobby, with a hand that clutched a brown, slightly worn leather briefcase containing some forms, Nicholas strode in and spotted Mrs Cerny in the corner.

"Please, follow me," Nicholas instructed gently.

They both stepped into a vast, but empty restaurant room. The curtains were drawn. The place looked dark, almost ghostly.

Nicholas and Mrs Cerny sat at a table, their matching, wooden chairs, fitted with dark green upholstery, in a salute to the sombre occasion. He took a pen and a slightly, crisp notepad out of his briefcase.

"Please can you repeat your name?" asked Nicholas.

"Berta Cerny," said Mrs Cerny.

"How did you get to Prague, Mrs Cerny?" inquired Nicholas.

"My husband used to be a politician. They forced us to escape from Sudetenland," explained Mrs Cerny.

"How old is your child?" asked Nicholas.

"My son is ten."

Nicholas wrote it down in his notebook. He looked up.

"I must be honest with you. I've learned of the situation through my friends. I'm not sure how, or even if, I can help. I'm sorry."

"I understand," said Mrs Cerny.

"Please wait for now. I will contact you if I can come up with anything to help," said Nicholas.

As Nicholas finished with Mrs Cerny, two women wandered in, both in their late thirties.

They approached Nicholas tentatively.

"Hello, my name is Adrianka Sykorka," the one introduced herself.

"And I am Bohdanka Hruska."

"Please help," said Mrs Sykorka.

Mrs Hruska interrupted her. "Can you send our children abroad?"

"How... how do you know me?" asked Nicholas.

"We hear your name from the people in the camp," said Mrs Sykorka.

Nicholas was at loss for words.

"I don't know what to say, however, I do appreciate you coming," said Nicholas.

"Our children are going to die," said Mrs Sykorka.

"My husband insists we send our children abroad," Mrs Hruska confirmed.

Nicholas nodded, as he processed his thoughts.

"What's your child's name? What's her age?" asked Nicholas.

"Irena. She is eleven years old," said Mrs Sykorka.

Nicholas turned to Mrs Hruska and waited on her answer.

"I have two boys, Hynek, and Janek, ten and eleven years old. They're very well—mannered boys," said Mrs Hruska.

"I'll see what I can do to help."

As the morning progressed, the table became covered with pieces of paper, with names scrawled on them. Nicholas was on his own, and he was reeling with the enormity of the need. Martin sauntered into the restaurant.

"What are you doing here so early?" asked Martin.

"Morning, Martin. You won't believe what happened," said Nicholas. "A desperate mother knocked on my door at six a.m."

"What on earth for?" said Martin perplexed.

"She wanted me to save her children. I did not know what to say to her."

"My goodness Nicholas…," exclaimed Martin.

"I have a few names already. I have to figure out a way to save these children," said Nicholas.

"Excellent, old chum…just bloody excellent! I knew you could help," said Martin, as he patted him on the shoulder.

"I didn't expect such a response from the people so fast."

"The word spreads quickly among refugees. Do you have a plan?" asked Martin.

"I'll gather as many names as possible and pray I can find a way to help them when I return to England," said Nicholas, as he showed the list of names to Martin.

"Plenty of children here. I have a hunch that many more are going to find their way to my doorstep for help."

"We need to get more people involved, more volunteers," said Martin.

"What about Tim?" asked Nicholas.

"He will help us, I am sure."

Later that evening, Nicholas sat in his hotel suite, looking out on the Prague night sky as the clock struck seven. The images he saw, haunted him as he cosied in the comfortable wooden armchair, almost the dark brown colour of the mud in the slums. He listened closely to the voice on the other side of the telephone, then spoke his mind.

"They want me to bring their children to England. Ma, I didn't have a clue what to say to these mothers. It's…it's horrible, just man forsaken awful but…. I want to help," explained Nicholas.

"There's a solution for everything," he repeated her words to himself.

He paused, "Thanks Ma…. Good night, Ma."

Chapter 5. Another Tough Morning

The next morning was a bitterly cold winter's morning. A knock on the door of Nicholas's suite door awoke him and he jumped out of bed, throwing on a bathrobe.

"Nicholas," whispered Martin.

Nicholas came up towards the door. When he slowly opened the door, he noticed Martin standing in front of the door, looking perplexed at him as he waved a piece of paper about.

"It's six—thirty and they are already here," said Martin with no preamble.

"Who?" said Nicholas.

"People…parents, children. They all want to put their children's names on the list," said Martin.

"Where are they?" asked Nicholas.

"Outside," said Martin.

It stunned Nicholas.

"Nicholas?" asked Martin.

"Yes?" asked Nicholas.

"It's freezing out there. You better hurry," said Martin.

"Ask them to wait in the restaurant. I'll be downstairs shortly," said Nicholas.

A few minutes later, Nicholas headed out of his room and as he arrived at the hotel lobby, he saw a dozen refugees standing in the restaurant, some poorly dressed, some not and all worried, all waiting at the table, urging to have their children taken away from them.

Pieces of blank paper lay on the table in the restaurant. Nicholas held something similar to a clipboard with forms attached. Next in line was Jaroslav Kocourek, who was in his mid—thirties.

"How old are your children?" asked Nicholas.

"Eight and nine," answered Jaroslav.

"Boys or girls?" asked Nicholas.

"A boy and a girl, Marek and Flora," said Jaroslav.

"Do they have any medical conditions?" asked Nicholas.

"Both are healthy, sir," said Jaroslav.

Nicholas handed over a form to Jaroslav, who surveyed it thoroughly.

"Please fill in the form. I'll contact you with more information," said Nicholas.

"When?" asked Jaroslav.

"Soon, hopefully."

"They took the children." A desperate mother shouted and, in a hurry, pushed in through the crowd, brandishing photos of her daughter.

"They took my neighbour's children. I am Milena Holub. Please! This is my daughter, Ester. She is only seven. Please, please, take her to England."

Nicholas looked up, surprised.

"I'll try," said Nicholas as he handed her a form.

"Please, Mrs Holub, please fill in the form," Nicholas gently instructed.

Milena backed away, tears running down her cheeks as she smiled and nodded graciously.

More refugees filled the room and Nicholas's face slacked with surprise, at the sheer volume of the need.

While Nicholas sat at the table, dealing with the refugees, Doreen and Tim walked in.

"Are you ready to get to work?" asked Nicholas.

"That's why I am here, my good man," said Tim.

He and Doreen sat at a nearby table.

"We can do it," said Nicholas.

"What's your plan?" asked Doreen, as she looked at Nicholas with respectful scepticism.

"Evacuate the children to England. As many as we can and find them families in England" explained Nicholas.

Doreen and Martin exchanged a look of surprise.

"Is this going to work, Nicholas?" asked Tim.

"We'll make it work," said Nicholas with firm determination.

"We can't just send thousands of children to England. They'll turn them away," Doreen retorted, not willing to trust the children to a plan that already had holes.

"I have to get permission from the Home Office, so the children can travel to England," said Nicholas.

"The Home Office will not help. Are you aware of that?" said Doreen, now standing with her hands on her hips, almost ready to walk out.

"Leave it to me."

Doreen heard the steel in his voice and despite the 'holes', found herself believing Nicholas could do it.

But she had to be sure and knew just what would test Nicholas's mettle. "I am visiting another camp this afternoon. Would you like to join me?"

With fine perception, Nicholas recognized the gauntlet, and with a firm resolve, he answered. "Yes, I would love to."

Doreen watched him for a moment and then nodded her assent. Nicholas looked down at the forms in his hand and gave a wry smile, having realized that no matter what lay ahead, his conscience, would now never allow him to turn back, from the path he had embarked on.

Chapter 6. Visiting the Refugee Zone

It was a bright afternoon, despite it being in the middle of winter. Nicholas, Doreen, and Martin stood in the middle of the slums, an overcrowded refugee zone, with the children in a most terrible state. They observed people in corrugated steel, tarnished huts, all gathered around a metal container, all shivering, as they tried to absorb the heat of the flames and warm up.

"How long have they all been here?" asked Nicholas, dismayed and sick to the core of his soul.

"Six or seven weeks. That's too long," replied Doreen, in a dead voice.

Nicholas looked at Doreen, at first stunned by her lack of emotion, but then suddenly understanding… it was because of her immense ability to feel, that she had to deaden her soul, which enabled her to work in such tragedy.

Nicholas approached Antonin and Barcinka Kotula, both in their thirties, as their child, Stanislav, rubbed his hands to keep them warm. Barcinka hugged herself to ward off the cold air that pressed into her skin.

"How long you have been here?" asked Nicholas.

"Eight weeks," replied Antonin.

"I want to help you," said Nicholas.

"Nobody can help us, sir," said Antonin, without rancour and hope.

"I would like to find a safe home for your child, a wonderful family somewhere in England. Would you allow us to take him if we can find a way?" asked Nicholas.

"No, no! He's, my boy!" said Barcinka, as she burst into tears, grabbing her son and shielding him away.

"He's not going anywhere! Who are you!? How dare you talk about taking my boy away?" said Barcinka, shielding her son even more.

"I understand your concern, however, please consider this opportunity. It might be his only chance to survive," pleaded Nicholas.

"Thank you," said Antonin.

"Please leave your details. I'll be in touch."

Antonin wrote the information on a form and gave it to Nicholas, amongst the pitiful cries of his wife.

Nicholas and Doreen walked off, having left a mother and father with an almost impossible decision to make.

"This place is worse than the last camp," said Nicholas.

"I am so glad you are here," Doreen suddenly answered, allowing a sliver of emotion to show. She had fought this battle alone for so long, that the genuine concern of another person almost disarmed her.

Nicholas nodded, deep in thought.

It was another late evening in Prague, and the dusk had long time blended into the night. Nicholas was unaware of time as he sat in the armchair in his hotel suite, perusing the photos of the children. Suddenly, the phone rang and pulled him out of his reverie. He picked it up and spoke.

"Hello…oh, hello Bob. How are you? I'm in the middle of something here. I have to stay in Prague for a bit longer. Some child welfare issues I am helping with. I need to be here right now. Yes, however, life is not only about making money. There are other priorities."

Nicholas quickly became irritated with his fickle colleague.

"I'm sure the good deals will still be there when I get back. For now, I have to stay here for a few more days. I'll come back as soon as I can. I'll let you know," Nicholas paused as he listened.

"Bob? After all, I've done for you?"

Nicholas hung up, intensely annoyed.

Early the following morning, Nicholas entered the hotel lobby, it was quiet and almost peaceful. Upon entering, he spotted Tim with Dalek Brozik, a thirty—year—old man, who appeared reserved, but dependable. One would assume he was an honest man too.

Tim and Dalek approached Nicholas.

"Nicholas, meet Dalek. He is here to help," said Tim.

Nicholas and Dalek shook hands.

"Good. I have to return to England. Can both of you continue with what I've started here?" asked Nicholas.

"Of course," said Tim.

Chapter 7. A Fairly Cold Morning

Three days later, on a cloudy and cold morning in London, Nicholas walked out of the terminal into a London, without the soul—stealing slums. Raindrops fell heavily on his face, but he was almost unaware of the wet cold. He walked towards a vast parking lot and headed for a line of black cabs, all waiting for a fare. He approached the very first cab and climbed into the rear of it.

"Home Office, please," Nicholas instructed the driver.

The cab driver drove away.

An hour later, the cabbie dropped Nicholas off at the Home Office. Nicholas paid his fare and walked into the Home Office. He noticed a receptionist, sitting behind the desk, squarely in front of a typewriter and he walked over to her.

"Good afternoon. I am here to speak with the Head of the Immigration Department," said Nicholas.

"Do you have an appointment?" asked the receptionist.

"No, it's important that I see someone today," insisted Nicholas.

"What is it regarding?" asked the receptionist.

"I want to know what paperwork, I would require to bring a child to England," said Nicholas.

"With their parents?" asked the receptionist.

"Unaccompanied."

"I am afraid that will not be possible," said the receptionist.

"Anything is possible. Can I see someone about this, please?" asked Nicholas convincingly.

The receptionist consulted her appointments book. "The earliest appointment I can give you is in four weeks."

"I don't have four weeks. I would like to see The Home Secretary instead," said Nicholas.

The receptionist scoffed

"Oh, really?" she retorted.

"Would you be kind enough to tell him I'm here?" asked Nicholas, undeterred.

"The Home Secretary is very busy. Besides, he wouldn't concern himself with such trivial business," said the receptionist.

Suddenly, a heavily pregnant woman walked past and fell to the floor. Nicholas rushed to her aid and helped her onto her feet.

"You will be fine," assured Nicholas, then he turned to the receptionist.

"She needs help. Call for an ambulance," said Nicholas.

The receptionist grabbed the phone, her hand shaking whilst holding the phone.

As soon as she finished the call, she came back over to assist, where Nicholas was standing with the pregnant woman. Nicholas made use of the moment granted to him and rushed across to the white—painted door and into the Home Secretary's office. As Nicholas burst in, he witnessed the Home Secretary, in his mid—sixties, putting a few golf balls into a makeshift hole.

The Home Secretary stood stunned by the unexpected intrusion.

"Who are you? Do you have an appointment?" asked the Home Secretary, clearly agitated.

"No, I don't have an appointment, however, I need your help, sir," said Nicholas, unflappable.

"Well then, how can I help?" asked the Home Secretary, sighing as he rubbed his hands in exasperation.

"I would like to bring unaccompanied Czechoslovakian children to England."

"And what does this have to do with England?" inquired the Home Secretary.

"Hitler is about to invade Czechoslovakia. There is an urgent need to help many children find new homes," explained Nicholas.

"That's very noble of you, but unfortunately, I won't be able to help without an appointment," said the Home Secretary, as he dismissed Nicholas and continued with his round of golf.

"Well, you know what I am seeking. I need an answer now. Will you help to save these children or not" demanded Nicholas.

"How dare you?! Leave at once! I most certainly have more important things to deal with," said the Home Secretary.

Nicholas lifted his eyebrow.

"Yes, well I can see just how busy you are with 'important things but I do insist on your answer now," he insisted.

"I have told you old chap. I'm busy."

"I can see that. Lovely swing you have there, sir," said Nicholas.

He carelessly threw an envelope onto the Home Secretary's elegant wooden desk.

"If you care more about children than you do about golf, you know what to do. My address is on the envelope," said Nicholas.

And with that, he turned around and walked out, with the Home Secretary staring at his retreating form in disbelief.

Chapter 8. Returning to Prague

By early that next week, Nicholas was back in Prague to continue with his mission. The restaurant had become his office and the table, his desk, was covered with papers. Nicholas sorted the children's files and photos, whilst Tim and Dalek focused on sipping soda.

"We have to act fast to help as many children as we can," said Nicholas.

"Agreed. We have to do our best," said Dalek.

The day began as more desperate parents arrived, quickly packing the room.

"How are you going to cope with all the paperwork, forms, and photographs?" asked Dalek.

"Patience and paperclips," Nicholas replied drily.

"The list of people is huge," said Dalek.

"And growing. I want to find homes for as many children as possible, perhaps even all of them," said Nicholas.

Tim glanced at a German—looking man sitting in the upper part of the restaurant, who gazed at them from behind a newspaper.

The man was Werner Hans, clad in an elegant suit, that belied his thirty—five years. Two Gestapo soldiers, also dressed in formal suits, flanked him.

Hans gazed at Dalek and Tim. Their eyes met.

"I believe we are being watched," observed Tim.

"Who is that man?" asked Nicholas.

"They look like German spies to me. Doreen said they followed her several times. We should move to my place, it's more discreet," suggested Tim.

"Brilliant idea," said Nicholas.

Hans stood up and pushed his way through the crowd. He reached for Nicholas with a fierce glare.

"What is this?" he shouted in German; irritation evident on his face.

He grabbed some forms and threw them in Nicholas's face.

"You better make sure what you're doing isn't against the interests of our Fuhrer," said Hans. He looked at Nicholas as he picked up the forms and waved them at Hans, as though he was wielding a fencing blade. His hand floated back and forth, up to Hans's face, then he retreated and moved forward, ready to attack.

"It's not your business what we do here," said Nicholas.

Hans flipped over the table. His two Gestapo soldiers threw chairs around and shoved people out of the way.

"It is my business! You don't tell me what I can do," yelled Hans.

"I have diplomatic immunity and political connections," said Nicholas.

The two Gestapo soldiers picked up more chairs and smashed them.

The restaurant manager forced himself through the crowd and approached, staring directly into Hans's eyes. "You have to leave the restaurant now. This is not a place for a social gathering!"

Hans backed off. "I will have my guys watching your back", he said, as he walked away with the two Gestapo soldiers following him.

In the dimly lit room of Nicholas's suite later that night, he sat at a desk laden with more papers and forms. When he had finally sorted out the papers, he stared at the phone in front of him. Picking up the handset, he dialled, intrigued to hear from his mother.

"Hello, Ma. Yes, all is well. Any news from the Home Office? Marvellous. So, they have answered my letter. Goodness me. That's fantastic news."

As he let his mother speak, he soon became worried.

"Oh, my word, what are the conditions to seek foster families? Sure, I can sort it out. Money, of course. It's always down to money. Fine, we'll find the money to cover the cost of travel."

Nicholas raised his shoulder.

"How much?! Fifty pounds?" He exclaimed, deflated.

"Fifty pounds is a lot of money."

He turned thoughtful.

"Fine, I'll find the money. Tim and Doreen are helping me. Most of these families cannot afford a meal, let alone a permit to travel abroad. I bet they cannot pay fifty pounds. I'll find the funds in England. Thank you, Ma. Have a good night," and with that, he hung up.

Guests filled the hotel restaurant. A party was in full swing. As the room swelled with more people and a welcoming atmosphere, Nicholas eyed a woman across the hall. He looked at a beautiful Swedish woman of about twenty years, that stood near the centre of the room, while she sipped from the wineglass in her hand. Clad in a glamorous dress, she drew every eye as she talked to hotel guests.

Nicholas approached her.

"What brings an attractive woman like you to this lovely city?" asked Nicholas.

"I am volunteering for the Red Cross, the Swedish branch."

"That's very interesting. Maybe you could help me?"

"I am not sure how?" said Lilly.

"There is a woman I met recently, a mother. She has got little time left, and she needs to send her children abroad. Her last wish is so she can die in peace, knowing her children are in safe hands," said Nicholas.

"It so happens, I am organising an evacuation of children to Sweden."

"Why are you going back to Sweden if there are more children which need help?" asked Nicholas.

"It's too risky here. The members of the Nazi Party are closely watching. No one can help such a huge number of children. At least, helping a few of them will make me fulfilled, that I've done something."

"Well, I would love to help you, find out what it is you do and learn something useful," said Nicholas, as he spotted Tim trying to catch his attention.

"Excuse me for a moment," said Nicholas.

Nicholas strode over to Tim.

"You don't know her," said Tim.

"She works for the Red Cross, Swedish branch."

"Could be a cover," said Tim.

"I like her. Trust me, she is fine. Besides, look at her. Isn't she gorgeous?"

"She does, and I am warning you, she may want to get close to those who help refugees flee the country. This could be bad news," advised Tim.

"There is nothing to worry about. She asked me to help her move some children to Sweden. I don't see a problem in that," said Nicholas, who returned to Lilly.

"What are you doing in Prague?" asked Lilly.

"I want to help the children. The more, the better."

"And how to do this? Are you an activist?" Lilly asked.

"No. Working as a stockbroker in London allowed me to build relationships with people, gaining their trust was important in my job. At the risk of sounding arrogant, I was good at it," said Nicholas.

Lilly smiled, batting her eyelashes. "Would you be willing to help me?" asked Lilly.

"I'll do my best," said Nicholas.

Early the next morning, Nicholas was sitting at the desk in his hotel suite, perusing the new pictures of children. He placed them aside and picked up an elegant fountain pen, with a sheet of paper and began to write a letter —

To the United States Embassy in London,

My name is Nicholas, and I am the Honorary Secretary of the British Committee for Refugees from Czechoslovakia, in charge of the Children's Department. I am contacting you regarding the dire situation in Czechoslovakia which calls for your urgent attention. My role is to seek new homes for hundreds of children in need of immediate transport to England.

I am asking for your help in this important matter.

Nicholas slipped the letter back into the envelope and put it aside.

Chapter 9. Visiting the Ruzyne Airport

The next morning at seven, Nicholas was standing at the Ruzyne airport in Prague, watching children and their anxious parents, as they waited on the tarmac path of the airport.

Whilst Lilly placed the early arriving children on the plane, Nicholas looked after the remaining children on the tarmac. Dobromira and her daughter, Paulina, stood next to Nicholas who instinctively comforted her son, Pavel.

Tim watched Hans and his two Gestapo soldiers, from across the tarmac.

"You're not afraid?" asked Tim.

"Afraid of what?" replied Nicholas.

He followed Tim's gaze and saw Hans and his men.

"They're watching us. They could arrest you and take you away for questioning," worried Tim.

"I'm British, and there is nothing to worry about. Besides, I am only saying goodbye to children," said Nicholas.

Tears in her eyes, Dobromira hugged both of her children. She knew this could be the last time she saw them and this made the emotional goodbyes, all the more bittersweet.

"My darlings," said Dobromira.

Nicholas turned to Paulina.

"Take care. Goodbye," said Nicholas.

A flight attendant dressed in an elegant outfit approached and took Paulina from Dobromira.

Nicholas put Pavel, who cried uncontrollably, on the ground. Dobromira hugged him as she glanced over at Hans, fearful for the lives of her children and herself.

Nicholas clocked Hans as he glared at Dobromira and Pavel.

"It's time for you to go. Come on, come on, go. Good luck!" said Nicholas to Pavel.

The flight attendant and Lilly took Paulina and Pavel onto the mid—sized plane.

At the top of the steps, Lilly waved Nicholas goodbye.

The plane door closed and the aircraft slowly departed.

Dobromira keened softly, as she watched her children jet off to safety. Nicholas stood listening to her broken heart that offered the ultimate sacrifice.

It was an early evening at the hotel bar. When the evening became less tense, Nicholas and Tim immersed themselves in sipping gin and tonics. Perched on high stools, they beamed with enthusiasm.

"Cheers! To the children and new beginnings," toasted Nicholas.

"Cheers," said Tim.

"This is proof anything reasonable can be done," said Nicholas.

"Absolutely. They'll have a new life in Sweden."

"It's only a matter of time before we find the money to get as many children as possible out of the country," said Nicholas, confidently, trying to forget the witness of Dobromira's pain.

It was a chilly night as Nicholas sat at his desk in his hotel suite. When he finally finished segregating the children's pictures, he sat back and let his thoughts run. With a smile, he remembered his promise to write his Ma, and with that, he reached for a pen and a sheet of paper —

Dear Ma, it's been busy here. The British Committee for Refugees is still trying to evacuate the children from Prague as soon as possible. I am very determined and I believe all things are possible. With the help of a representative of the Red Cross, we've transported the first twenty children to Sweden.

I feel compelled to set up a children's section in London. If Hitler invades Europe, all citizens will be in imminent danger. There will be no hope for any of the refugees. I am looking forward to finding foster families as soon as I can. I'll see you on Saturday afternoon. Lots of love, your son, Nicholas.

Chapter 10. The Telegram

Just after nine, the next morning, just as Nicholas entered the hotel lobby in a bit of a rush, the receptionist leapt to her feet and called out for Nicholas.

"Mr Nicholas! Mr Nicholas!" He heard his name echo throughout the lobby.

Nicholas instinctively turned around and stopped, "Yes…how can I help?"

"There is a telegram for you," the receptionist replied.

"Oh, who is it from?" asked Nicholas.

"It came from Sweden," said the receptionist.

She handed Nicholas the telegram.

Nicholas took out a letter from the inner compartment of his jacket. "Could you send this letter for me, please?"

"Certainly, sir."

Nicholas passed a letter over to the receptionist. "Thank you."

Nicholas checked the telegram. It read: 'CHILDREN ARRIVED SAFELY. LILLY.'

A big smile formed on Nicholas's face.

Excited, Nicholas entered the restaurant and hurried over to Tim, who was waiting at a table.

"The children have arrived safely in Sweden," announced Nicholas.

"Splendid news," said Tim.

"Listen, I must go back to England. I need you to take care of the transport logistics here. Can you do that?" asked Nicholas.

"Giving up the fight?" Tim questioned him.

"Good heavens, no. I'm going back to find as many foster families as possible for the children," said Nicholas, as Tim's face lit up.

"Don't worry about anything in Prague. I'll take care of everything," said Tim.

"You can't send any children to England until I've found homes for them."

"Oh, I am sure you'll do well," said Tim.

"Not so sure. People aren't always this generous," worried Nicholas.

"Until they meet you."

They both laughed.

"Thank you for your confidence in me, Tim," said Nicholas.

Tim poured wine into their glasses, as both of them smiled at the good fortune of their unlikely friendship.

Chapter 11. Returning Home
After New Year's Eve in Prague

It was an early afternoon in London and as Nicholas walked up to the house in London, he felt the drizzling rain dance off his nose. But nothing could deter his mood, he was home. As he walked up the path, he looked through the window and spotted his mother in front of the cooking hob.

Nicholas walked into the kitchen.

"Hello Ma," said Nicholas.

"Nicholas, I'm so glad you're back."

Nicholas hugged and kissed his mum.

"The dinner is ready whenever you are hungry."

"Thank you, Ma. I've been thinking…I need a secretary to set up an organization to help the children once they arrive in England."

"I could help," she replied.

"Goodness me. Lovely of you, mother, but I care about your health more."

"I'm well enough."

"Doctor's orders. You must rest, you can supervise my secretary if you wish," said Nicholas as he grinned.

Barbara smiled back. "Do you have anybody in mind?"

"Erm…no. Not yet."

"How about Kate? She's a very pleasant lady," she suggested.

Nicholas grinned.

"What would I do without you?" asked Nicholas.

"You'd manage splendidly."

Just after nine the next morning, Nicholas walked into the spacious lobby of a busy London Stock Exchange centre. Dressed to impress, he approached the receptionist, Kate Lewis, a woman in her mid—thirties, as she sipped her favourite coffee, which boosted her concentration.

"Nicholas! How was your holiday?" asked Kate enthusiastically.

"It's been really busy. Is Bob in today?" inquired Nicholas.

Bob passed by.

"Nicholas, you are late," admonished Bob.

"The traffic was horrendous," explained Nicholas.

"I am glad you are back. Now come on, get onto the floor," said Bob.

"Of course," said Nicholas, and he turned to Kate. "We need to talk."

"In your own time, Nicholas," said Kate.

Nicholas rushed off to the trading floor.

Later that afternoon, just as five o'clock struck, Nicholas rushed down the road in London, to reach his apartment. Kate Lewis waited for him, holding a paper cup in her hand. She was sipping her favourite coffee, while she waited for Nicholas, as well as, enjoying the splendid sunshine that the pleasant afternoon offered.

"Apologies for being late," said Nicholas.

"Don't worry about that. How was your first day back?" asked Kate.

"Busy as usual. I had to catch up," said Nicholas.

Nicholas opened the door, "After you." Then, he hung his coat on the wooden coat rack. Kate took off her hat and coat and handed them to Nicholas as he hung them on the coat rack.

"Shall we proceed?" asked Nicholas.

He ushered Kate into a reception room filled with dark wooden desks and other memorabilia. Fencing weapons hung on the wall, with pictures all over the place.

Kate observed her surroundings, as she glanced upon the photographs and trophies.

"Interesting. All yours?" asked Kate.

"They are, indeed."

At his desk, Nicholas pulled out the top drawer and took out a notebook with names.

Kate continued to peruse the photographs, many of them showing Nicholas fencing at various tournaments or holding various trophies. She turned to Nicholas.

"Very impressive. How many prizes did you win?" Kate asked.

"Not sure. It was fun, to be honest, nothing serious," said Nicholas.

"Do you still do it?" she asked.

"Occasionally, with Bob," replied Nicholas.

"You should continue doing what you are good at," advised Kate.

"I might not fence seriously anymore. I started a fencing event involving cadets from all over the country. My mission is to make sure fencing will continue for decades," explained Nicholas.

"That's very noble," said Kate.

Nicholas gave Kate a shy smile. "Well then, there is a lot of work ahead. Shall we make a start?"

"Certainly."

Later, Kate looked through documents and photographs of children. While she did her best to allocate the photographs, Nicholas wrote on an envelope — *To US Embassy, 1 Grosvenor Square, London, W1.*

"We haven't received a response from the US Ambassador. He may not be aware of how important this is," said Nicholas.

"If you make him understand children's lives depend on his decision, he might respond," said Kate.

"He'd better hurry. We're running out of time," said Nicholas.

Nicholas grabbed a piece of paper and wrote —
Dear US Ambassador,

I am writing to update you on the situation in Czechoslovakia. Thousands of children and their parents evacuated to Prague. The situation is getting worse each day. I have written to you already, however, I haven't received a reply. This time, I am writing to remind you of the importance of saving children at risk. I need your help! I pray for your prompt help in this matter.

As Nicholas browsed through some photographs, Kate stacked all the letters, they had written on the desk.

"We need to reach as many families as possible," said Nicholas.

"There must be plenty of families willing to adopt a child. What about countries other than America?" asked Kate.

"Still waiting to hear from the embassies, though I am not sure this will be successful," said Nicholas.

"No harm in reaching out to them," she said.

"You're right."

Later that evening in London, as the clocks were about to strike nine, Nicholas was still hard at work at his desk, as he opened an envelope and took out official documents, forms, ID samples and stamps.

Kate browsed through a bunch of blank ID papers and official stamps.

"What is it? Are they fakes?" she asked.

"It's what we need to get us going," said Nicholas.

"Where did you get all of this from?" asked Kate.

"I have contacts," he said.

"That's convenient," said Kate.

Nicholas paused, reflecting on whether to share everything with Kate.

"I am well—connected in the British establishment," he whispered.

Kate looked askance.

"Spies abound in the Establishment.'

Chapter 12. Returning Home After Working at the Stock Exchange

A few days later Nicholas arrived at the house in London after he visited the Stock Exchange. He met Kate standing in front of the entrance. As Nicholas opened the door, Kate picked up the letters off the floor and not wasting any time, they moved on to work.

Nicholas wrote a letter whilst Kate went through the mail.

As she opened an envelope with an official stamp of the US Embassy, she beamed with joy.

"My goodness!" she exclaimed.

Nicholas looked up, puzzled. Kate showed him a letter.

"It's an invitation to speak with the American Ambassador himself."

Nicholas radiated with joy. "At last!"

At ten the next morning, Nicholas rushed to the headquarters of the US Embassy. He walked confidently towards the reception.

"Ambassador's office, please."

"Down the hallway, the first door to the right," replied a middle—aged receptionist.

Nicholas knocked on the wooden door.

"Come in," said the US Ambassador.

Nicholas walked in, his eyes focused on the ambassador, seated in front of the desk.

"Please sit down," he said.

Nicholas sat across from the ambassador.

The US Ambassador put a smile on his face and then leant forward.

"Mr Winton, thank you for coming. I have invited you here to speak with you in person."

"I am pleased you did because it's a matter which requires urgent action," said Nicholas.

The US Ambassador adjusted his tone of voice.

"I appreciate your efforts. It's very charitable of you, and because of the lack of immigration laws appropriate to this matter, the relocation of children in the numbers requested would be impossible."

"A small country like Sweden came forward to help, and yet a powerful country like the United States of America is unwilling to help? This makes no sense," replied Nicholas, utterly disappointed.

"Unfortunately, it would take too much time to pass new immigration laws," said the US Ambassador.

"It's so unfair. These are helpless children," said Nicholas.

"I hear you, Mr Winton. However, considering the circumstances, there is not much I can do," said the Ambassador.

"There are thousands of children and parents, all of them hopeless. Such a powerful country like America cannot stand by and do nothing."

"Mr Winton, it would take time to change our laws on immigration," said the US Ambassador.

"So, what are you going to do about the children?" demanded Nicholas.

"I am afraid, there is nothing I can do," said the US Ambassador.

It disappointed Nicholas more than he believed it could and a heaviness settled on him.

As the early morning blended into the haze of the afternoon, the weather in Prague became exceedingly pleasant. In a small, nondescript building, where Doreen's office was situated, Tim sat at an old, wooden desk and wrote a telegram. On the other side of the room, Dalek just sat behind the desk, thoughtful.

"Money has gone missing. Do you know anything about that?" asked Tim.

"Oh my goodness, no, what do you want me to do?" said Dalek.

Tim turned suspicious.

"I have to inform Nicholas."

"Of course," said Dalek.

Tim dragged the typewriter toward him and typed away: "TRANSPORT POSTPONED, PROBABLY TUESDAY. NEED MORE MONEY."

Chapter 13. The Rescue Mission
Running at Full Speed

In London, the afternoon turned into evening, and the evening into the dark of night, and yet the work continued. A large, brown, framed board covered with children's photos lay against the wall and papers were strewn all across the room. Hundreds of application forms lay in piles on the desk.

Nicholas grabbed the telephone and dialled.

"Tim?! I got your telegram. How are things going over there? That's good. And how is Doreen? Why? What happened? Where did she go?"

A long silence. Worry spread all over Nicholas's face.

"They placed her on the Gestapo list. Is she safe? That's good. She made the right decision."

A beat.

"Right, I'll be sending money soon. Meanwhile, I need you to get the names of those Slovakian boys and distract the attention of the Gestapo as best you can. No, it's not a problem. It's the conditions laid out by the Home Office that is the problem."

Nicholas closed the folder and headed off towards his bed.

Another day in London, with shelves filled with more folders. Pieces of papers with children's names covered the walls. Documents and applications were all over the desk and the floor, leaving Nicholas and Kate just enough space to sit in front of the desk.

"To find families or guarantors willing to pay fifty pounds will be an uphill struggle. Many families have problems of their own. Some can barely look after themselves. We need to talk to the Home Office to make them understand," said Kate.

"They will not budge. I know them," worried Nicholas.

He grabbed a folder filled with photographs.

"If you want to place a child, you need to advertise it," said Nicholas, as he mulled the idea over in his head.

"Nicholas, what are you talking about?" asked Kate.

"In business, you present the product first and then advertise it well," explained Nicholas.

"That's not right," said Kate.

"No, it is just right. We must treat this as a business transaction. We have to advertise the idea, get the attention of families and close the deal. It will work, perfect marketing sense," promised Nicholas.

Nicholas walked into the newspaper office. After he entered the building, he faced the receptionist and the manager, a man in his forties.

"Forty pounds for an ad, it's far over my budget," said Nicholas.

"I understand your position, but we have to keep the price up. There are a lot of businesses out there willing to pay the price," explained the manager.

Nicholas contemplated the news.

"What if I write you a front—page article about the political situation in the Sudetenland and the families and their children starving, who need immediate help?"

The manager considered the option, "That's something I could consider. I'll need to have it ready before ten p.m."

"I'll have it done," reassured Nicholas.

Nicholas grabbed an out—of—date version of the newspaper and hurried out.

Although it was a late night at the house in London, the lights were still on, as Nicholas sat at the desk and typed away. Kate stood behind him, looking over his shoulder as he re—considered the content of the poster.

"Adopt a Child," said Nicholas.

"How about 'Give a Home to a Child'?" suggested Kate.

"Perfect," said Nicholas.

Nicholas left the house and walked off to the newspaper stand to pick up the latest print, enjoying the cloudy day.

The headline screamed: 'GIVE A HOME TO A CHILD!'

He walked away with a big smile on his face.

On the way back, Nicholas stopped off at the local church. He unrolled a poster and stuck it to the wall of the church.

It said: 'GIVE A HOME TO A CHILD!'

Chapter 14. The Dark Shadows of the Streets of Prague

Dalek walked out of Doreen's office in Prague and headed down the alleyway. Hans appeared out of the darkness and approached him. Together with Hans was Heinrich Schulter, a tall man in his forties. Their rough looks and Gestapo uniforms told a lot about the men and Dalek knew his very life hung by a thread.

"Do you have the money?" asked Schulter.

"Here," stuttered Dalek as he slipped the envelope to Schulter who opened it and quickly counted the money. "Not enough. Next time I'll need more."

Dalek was shocked.

"Think about your wife and daughter," advised Schulter.

"I will. They're the most important to me," said Dalek.

"Doreen Warner… is she involved in this?" asked Hans.

"She…is….," said Dalek.

Hans showed a cruel, forbidding face, that did not bode well for Doreen.

"Good. Off you go, now."

Dalek stood undecided…gravelly concerned with the implications of his actions.

"Hear me? Go home!" ordered Hans.

As he shoved Dalek, Dalek turned and scurried away to safety.

Darkness shrouded the town. Clouds of tiny water droplets hung in the atmosphere. Dalek strode through the mist and reached his small, rundown house. He let himself into his house, took off his jacket and hat, headed over to something similar to a baby cot and kissed his baby girl.

His wife Adele Brozik, a handsome woman in her thirties, walked into the room.

"Did you give money to the Gestapo again?" asked Adele.

"I had to," said Dalek with his head down, ashamed of his actions, yet caught in a trap he felt he could not escape from.

"We can't live like this!"

"We have no other choice. What about our daughter?" asked Dalek.

"What about those children? There are a lot of them. They won't be able to send them out of the country without money," said Adele.

"I have no choice, I have to put us first," said Dalek.

"This extortion has to stop."

Dalek slammed his fist against the wall.

"I have to do what I am asked until I find a way of saving us!"

Chapter 15. Looking for Foster Parents

It was an early evening on the streets of a swanky building estate, in a busy street in the Kensington area, London. Nicholas knocked on a door, with no answer. He knocked... again and again, until, Mary Jones, in her mid—sixties, opened the door. Nicholas stood before her, professionally decked out and with a smile on his face.

"Good evening, madam. Are you aware of the political situation in Czechoslovakia at the moment?" asked Nicholas.

"Vaguely," said Mary.

"Hundreds of children are at risk of being persecuted by the members of the Nazi Party," said Nicholas.

"It's terrible over there," agreed Mary.

Nicholas reached for his catalogue and opened it. Mary glanced at the children's photographs.

"It's their fault," said Mary.

"I'm sorry?" asked Nicholas, thoroughly astounded.

"Czechoslovakians are to blame for their situation," asked Mary.

"These are only vulnerable children."

"As long as Czechoslovakians are with the Nazi Party, they'll be to blame," said Mary.

Nicholas moved on down the street and approached another mansion. He knocked and knocked again.

Jonathan Smith, a man in his forties and quite rotund stood on his doorstep, with a strong posture, very military—like. When Nicholas quickly picked up the mood of the man, he put on his best smile and presented his pitch.

"My wife couldn't handle it. She just had a miscarriage. It would upset her," said Jonathan.

"How so? Maybe another child might pull her out of her melancholy?" suggested Nicholas.

"It would be too emotionally devastating for her. So no, the answer is no!" said Jonathan.

"Fine, so that you know. I will be back here tomorrow, talking to your neighbours, and your wife might get wind of you deciding for her, without her knowing. She might get furious at you. You should probably talk to your wife right now to make sure she agrees with you," advised Nicholas.

"Excuse me! Leave now, right now…" said Jonathan, with a touch of aggression in his tone.

"I am trying to save your marriage," insisted Nicholas.

"Leave my wife out of it," warned Jonathan.

"Jonathan? What is happening?" asked Jonathan's wife Barbara, a tender woman in her mid—thirties. Chloe, all of five years, clung to her mother's leg.

Barbara gazed at Nicholas and then at her husband. "Who is this?"

"Good evening, madam. I brought some pictures with me. If you would look at them?"

"You don't have to," said Jonathan.

Nicholas quickly handed her his catalogue. Barbara browsed through it.

"Does this girl deserve this type of life?" asked Nicholas, gently.

Barbara's eyes fill up with tears. "Goodness, no, of course not."

"You have a beautiful daughter," said Nicholas.

"Thank you."

Nicholas handed her the form.

"Please consider adopting a child and save a child's life," insisted Nicholas.

Barbara stared at her husband.

"We'd accept a child if it means saving their life. I would love another child," said Barbara.

Jonathan smiled.

"We could take a child, couldn't we?" asked Barbara. "I've been longing for a child for long now."

"Yes," replied Jonathan.

"We should take two, shouldn't we?" Barbara continued.

"They would be more than welcome in our house," confirmed Jonathan.

Nicholas grinned from ear to ear.

Nicholas moved on. He walked towards another house. He knocked on the door... and again, this time harder. Nicholas showed his catalogue to the landlord, a Northerner in his mid—forties.

"Hundreds of children were evacuated from Prague," explained Nicholas.

"This must be illegal, surely," said the landlord.

"Not at all, sir. The Home Office has given its assent. These children are in imminent danger. We need to move them somewhere where they will be safe," affirmed Nicholas.

"This might not be the best time. My wife has passed away. I'll be moving up North as soon as I sell my house. Besides, what is the Czechoslovakian government doing about it?" asked the landlord.

"The government already does its best to help, and it appears they cannot do much. You could support the mission financially. Fifty pounds would cover the cost of transporting and housing a child."

"My goodness. Fifty pounds!?" exclaimed the landlord.

"That's the amount the Home Office requires for each child," said Nicholas.

The landlord thought it over.

"What you're doing is great. I truly admire your efforts."

Nicholas handed over the form to the landlord and smiled then he moved on and kept his smile fixed as he knocked on the next door. This time, Gerd, a man of light hair, fair skin and blue eyes, in his mid—forties, opened the door. Nicholas put on his best smile but he was starting to feel his strength wane, the constant optimism was exhausting.

"What's your opinion of the current state of affairs in Europe? In Czechoslovakia…" asked Nicholas, as his eyes moved to a swastika flag hanging on the wall in the hall.

Gerd leered at Nicholas.

"I think you're going to want to slam the door in my face," said Nicholas.

Gerd slammed the door in Nicholas's face.

The clocks in London struck ten and the witching hour was just around the corner. Nicholas put photographs of the children into a folder marked, 'Adopted Children'. As he did so, Kate watched him, whilst sipping her tea.

Nicholas looked up at her.

"Has anyone shown interest in adopting that girl yet?" asked Nicholas.

"No, not yet," said Kate.

"That's not good," worried Nicholas.

"How can we know those families can look after these children? Maybe having someone who can vet the families would be a good thing?" suggested Kate.

"Good idea," said Nicholas.

Nicholas inspected some more photographs and documents.

"What's wrong?" asked Kate.

"The Home Office is too slow. I'll need to fake some more documents," said Nicholas.

"You are playing with fire," warned Kate.

"What's illegal? Letting children die or forging papers? As long as it works, we do it," said Nicholas.

"Can't say I disagree. We are not against the Home Office. We are against the Nazis," said Kate.

"We have to do the best we can without what we got," said Nicholas.

Kate cut out photos of the children.

"Chop—chop, the job is done."

Nicholas glued the photos to ID cards and travel documents and stamped the official papers with a fake stamp. Kate then placed them in envelopes.

"I am still concerned about those Jewish boys from the eastern part of Czechoslovakia," said Kate.

"They may not take the train from Prague. They would need to travel to Lovosice train station and board from there. I am going to inform their father myself," said Nicholas.

Nicholas looked tired.

"I better go. You need to get some sleep," said Kate.

"You are right, I've not been sleeping properly since I started this," admitted Nicholas.

As the long evening came to the end, Nicholas grabbed Kate's jacket off the light wooden coat rack and handed it to her, helping her put it on.

"It's late. Thank you for today. You did well," said Nicholas.

"Good night, Nicholas."

Chapter 16. Listening to Incoherent Treats

It was a late night in Prague, as the clocks struck ten. Hitler ranted on the radio and an atmosphere of fear permeated the one—family house. Lidka and Alojz Zmolek, in their thirties, sat at a wobbly table, their eyes focused on eight—year—old Rudolf, as they spoke Czech.

"Son, we have to tell you something," said Alojz.

"What is it?" asked Rudolf.

"You are going to England," said Lidka.

"When?" asked Rudolf.

"This Saturday. You'll take the train to meet uncle Shimon," said Alojz.

"We'll have a little party to celebrate you leaving," said Lidka.

"Are you coming with me?"

"We'll join you soon," promised Alojz.

Lidka hugged her son as tears ran down her cheeks.

"Why? Are you trying to get rid of me?" asked Rudolf.

"Of course not. We need you to stay with uncle Shimon…only temporarily," said Alojz.

"I don't want to go. I want you to come with me," said Rudolf.

"Listen, Rudolf. It's the safest choice right now," said Alojz.

"Why are you sending me away?" asked Rudolf, as tears also welled up in his eyes.

"You'll have fun with uncle Shimon. He is going to show you England," said Lidka.

"I can only speak Czech," worried Rudolf.

"Uncle Shimon will sign you up for English classes, and you'll make new friends," said Lidka.

Lidka stood up and walked off, unable to stem the flood of tears that overwhelmed her. She took a piece of material and started to sew a piece of clothing for her son.

Chapter 17. The Rescue
Mission Continues

The following day, when the early night had already blended into the early morning and with clouds that hung heavily over London, Nicholas walked into the Home Office. He headed towards the reception area and as the receptionist looked up from her typewriter, he asked. "May I meet with the Home Secretary, please?"

"What is it regarding?" inquired the receptionist.

"It's about the Czechoslovakian children. It's a very urgent matter," said Nicholas.

"Give me a moment, please," said the receptionist.

The receptionist arose and disappeared into a nearby office. Nicholas started to feel impatient, there was so much to do and so little time to do it in.

The elderly receptionist returned.

"Unfortunately, the Home Secretary isn't available at the moment. He is in the middle of a very important meeting," said the receptionist.

"Could you inform him that the children's visas haven't arrived yet?" asked Nicholas.

"I'll pass on the message," said the receptionist.

Nicholas left the office, deeply perturbed by the Home Office's nonchalance, but determined not to give up. He waited outside the Home Office. He gazed upon the Home Secretary as he walked out together with a few other Home Office workers. As they started to go their separate ways, Nicholas ran over to the Home Secretary.

"Excuse me, Sir," said Nicholas.

"Goodness, not you again," groaned the Home Secretary.

"Sir, I am waiting for the children's visas. Why haven't they come?" demanded Nicholas.

"I am afraid my schedule is tight. There is not much we can do to speed up the process," said the Home Secretary.

"You know his matter is very urgent. We need them as soon as possible," insisted Nicholas.

"I'll speak with our Immigration Services about it, but I cannot make any promises. Bye for now," said the Home Secretary as he walked off, leaving Nicholas at a loss.

Early evening in London as Nicholas pored through the files again.

Something worried him and he turned to Kate. "Permits are missing. Visas haven't arrived yet. The staff at the Home Office have moved at a snail's pace," he complained.

"What are we going to do?" asked Kate.

"We have to print the visas ourselves."

"Are you crazy? We will go to jail," said Kate.

"There is no other solution. We need to act now. If they can't do it, we'll have to do it ourselves," said Nicholas.

He opened a box and took out some counterfeit travel documents and visas.

Kate stood in shock.

"Plenty of those on the black market," said Nicholas with a grin.

"Oh my God, Nicholas. I can't be part of this."

"We'll use them until the Home Office gets its act together," said Nicholas.

Kate thought long and hard of the consequences.

"I guess it's for the children."

"That's right. For their new start in life," said Nicholas.

Chapter 18. Bitterly Cold Evening in Prague

In Prague, it was nine on a bitterly cold evening. Dana Matas, in her mid—thirties, washed the dishes and dried them with a cloth. At the kitchen table was Gabriel Matas, her husband, just a few years older than her, sat thoughtfully as he gazed at his daughter Agata. She was seven years old and had taken over the reading of a Czech children's storybook.

"Was school fine?" Gabriel asked Agata.

The girl stopped reading, raised her head and looked towards her father, with grave concern.

"It was fine, but soldiers came today," said Agata.

"Soldiers!? What soldiers? What did they do?" asked Gabriel, alarmed.

"They were shouting loud. They took down all the pictures hanging on the wall. Everyone got scared, they also put a picture of a man with a weird toothbrush moustache instead. Then, a boy was crying. They called him a Jew and asked him to sit in the last row," said Agata.

"What? And what did the teacher do?" asked Gabriel.

"Mrs Svoboda said, from now on, the best children sit at the back of the class," said Agata.

Concerned, Gabriel turned to Dana.

"We should find another school for her," said Gabriel.

"It would be better to send her to England. They have excellent schools there," said Dana.

"Surely not England, definitely somewhere closer," said Gabriel.

"We could all move to England," suggested Dana.

"I am too old to move to a new country. I don't want to start all over again. This is my home," said Gabriel.

"We could send her first until it is all over," said Dana.

"What if it's not over soon?" asked Gabriel.

Dana looked into her husband's eyes and spoke a thousand words to his heart, as Gabriel reached out to hug her.

"I want my daughter to be safe. We have to send her first for her safety," insisted Dana.

Another late evening in London as Kate stared at an envelope and Nicholas peeked out of the window, thoughtful and pensive.

"The children's visas have arrived," said Kate.

"I hope they won't notice the forged documents," said Nicholas.

"I hope so too," said Kate.

"We will exchange them for genuine ones when the children arrive in England," said Nicholas.

Back in Prague. Doreen and Tim get the documents ready. Nicholas walks into Doreen's office.

"Are all the documents ready?" asked Nicholas.

"Ready for tomorrow," confirms Tim.

Chapter 19. Final Goodbyes

The following day, at the Wilson Train Station in Prague, was quieter than usual as the station clock struck seven—fifteen. Nicholas and Tim were standing on the platform with the light breeze blowing the morning chill over their skin. There was a taint of fear and apprehension in the air as they watched the parents and children. The final goodbye was coming. Children were clutching small suitcases, with special passes that hung around their necks, with their photos and numbers on. Some girls held dolls and other boys clutched teddy bears.

Dana Matas arranged her daughter Agata's pass to ensure it was visible.

"Keep it safe. It's important the family in England recognises you," said Dana.

Gabriel Matas held Agata's chin to speak to her.

"We are looking forward to visiting you and your new family soon. Don't worry about us. We'll be fine. Enjoy your holiday," said Gabriel.

Dana and Gabriel held their tears in check, there would be time later to free their emotions.

"When your name gets checked off, please proceed to the other side," instructed Tim.

Nicholas turned to Agata. "You'll have a good life there in England. I promise."

Tim and Nicholas moved to Rudolf and his parents, Lidka and Alojz.

"What is your name?" asked Tim.

Rudolf stops smiling.

"Rudolf," he replied.

Tim ticked Rudolf's name off the list.

"You'll be in expert hands," promised Lidka.

"Uncle Shimon will look after you," said Alojz.

Their words and actions worried Rudolf, who was tearful.

Lidka squeezed Rudolf in her arms. "All will be well, my boy."

Next Nicholas and Tim were with Zdenka and Dominik Cibulka and their two daughters Ada, seven years old and Kristina nine years old.

Nearby, Hans and some Gestapo officers watched the entire process.

"What are your names?" asked Nicholas.

"Ada Cibulka," replied Ada.

"My name is Kristina Cibulka," said Kristina.

Nicholas turned to Tim. "Kristina is not on our list."

"We need our daughter to go, please," said Zdenka.

"If she's not on our list, she can't go," said Tim resolutely.

"I want my sister to come with me," mumbled Ada, as tears filled her eyes.

"I am sorry. We couldn't find a family to look after your sister," explained Nicholas.

"Please. You can do this. Please, she must go," begged Dominik.

"I understand how you feel, sir. Unfortunately, we couldn't find a foster family for your daughter. She'll have to travel another time," said Nicholas.

"Please! I want to go with my sister," cried Kristina. "Please let me go?"

She started to cry pitifully.

"You'll have to wait. You are older and far stronger than your sister. We have to let Ada go first," said Nicholas.

Suddenly, the train arrived, with a scream and a rush of steam.

Hans and the Gestapo Officers tensed up.

The crowd started to become restless. For many, this would be the final goodbye.

As Dominik set Ada onto the train, Kristina stared at her sister through the window, a piece of glass the only barrier between two sibling hearts. Tears ran down both their faces and their hands touched through the glass.

Zdenka approached the window and as she hugged Ada, she almost pulled her halfway out. Dominik rushed over.

"Don't…she must go!" said Dominik.

He pushed Ada back onto the train as Zdenka let her go, having lost the battle to reign in her tears.

"Be good. We'll be there soon," said Dominik.

Dominik reached into his pocket, took out a picture of Moses, and gave it to Ada.

"Keep this one with you," said Dominik.

He turned the picture over and pointed at the Ten Commandments.

"When scared, pray to Moses," said Dominik.

Through a sheen of tears, Zdenka gave Ada a notebook.

"This is for you, keep it. I want you to write about it every day. You'll read it to us when we come to see you," said Zdenka.

The train whistle blew as steam billowed and filled the air around the train. The train was about to set off.

Ada's eyes were focused on her sister.

"Papa, I want Kristina to come with me," pleaded Ada.

Dominik handed ten German marks to Kristina.

"Keep this. Hold it tight," said Dominik.

Kristina held it in her hand.

Dominik lifted Kristina to the window. Both girls hugged each other. "Look after Ada."

He then pushed Kristina onto the slowly departing train.

Nicholas watched the tragic goodbye and hurried over as he realized what Dominik was doing.

"Stop! She is not allowed!" yelled Nicholas.

He grabbed Kristina and held her tight in his arms.

Nicholas turned to Dominik. " You can't do that! You put her at risk. They will turn her away if she arrives in London without papers, do you understand?"

"I want to go with Ada to look after her," said Kristina.

"You'll go next time, I promise. I'll find a family for you in the same town as Ada," said Nicholas.

Kristina looked into Nicholas's eyes and saw the truth of his words and with that, she smiled at Ada, with waves of kisses.

The train departed.

Hans and his Gestapo officers approached Nicholas as he stood back, wary of their intentions.

"We meet again," said Hans.

Hans glanced at the train, and then back at Nicholas.

"Sending children out of the country?" asked Hans.

"It's a school trip to Slovakia," said Nicholas.

"Don't lie to me!" barked Hans.

"They'll be back soon," said Nicholas.

Hans glared at Nicholas with pure hatred in his eyes. Then he turned around and stormed off the platform. Nicholas watched him and slowly sighed.

Nicholas and Doreen sat in the office in Prague. Tim stood by the wooden window, looking out. Although all three of them appeared tired, they seemed very relieved with the turn of events.

"We were so lucky," said Tim.

"Good thing you came to help," said Doreen.

"Thanks to all of you. I have to go back to London to continue our work. We will plan the next evacuation better. The Gestapo's everywhere now. We must act before they arrest us or…," said Nicholas.

Nicholas stopped himself as Doreen and Tim stared at him.

"Or what?" asked Doreen.

"Kill us," said Nicholas.

Doreen and Tim took in the full impact of Nicholas's words.

"You're free to leave, of course. What we are doing might be worth death at the hands of barbarians," said Nicholas.

Suddenly, Doreen looked defiant.

"We have more and more Slovakian families approaching us. Could you find more English homes for them?" asked Doreen.

"And more people to fork out fifty pounds for each child?" asked Tim.

Nicholas smiled.

"I may well do," said Nicholas.

At the window, Tim looked at Dalek, who stood across the street, as he talked to Hans and the Gestapo Officers. Tim turned to Nicholas and Doreen, who looked at him suspiciously.

"What?" asked Doreen.

"Dalek is out there talking with the Gestapo," said Tim.

"They always threaten me too. Dalek is tough. He'll ignore them," said Doreen.

Moments later, while Tim and Doreen tidied their desks, Nicholas sat, going through a file.

German soldiers burst through the door. Hans and Schulter marched in, followed by the Gestapo Officers.

"Passports!" shouted Schulter.

German Soldiers searched the office.

"What passports?" asked Nicholas.

Without a warning, Hans slapped Nicholas hard.

Nicholas staggered back, dazed, that Hans would dare.

Doreen grabbed several travel permits and stuffed them into her underwear. She rushed into the bathroom as Hans spoke to Nicholas, but he saw her sudden move.

Doreen locked herself in the bathroom and tore the permits into pieces. She quickly flushed them down the toilet, as Hans banged on a wooden door.

"Open the door!" shouted Hans in German.

BANG! BANG!

Doreen tore and flushed, then tore some more and flushed. Working deftly, knowing the very lives in the passports, depending on her actions.

The door smashed open and Hans exploded into the room. He grabbed Doreen and dragged her out.

Gestapo Officers threw the desk upside down and papers landed all over the floor.

"Get out!" shouted Nicholas.

Hans spat into Nicholas's face and then signalled to his comrades. Soon, the Gestapo Officers dragged Nicholas out of the building.

"What are you doing in Prague?" asked Hans.

"I am visiting a friend. He needs help to open a business in London," replied Nicholas.

Hans spat at Nicholas again.

"Our Fuhrer is the ruler now. If you work against our Fuhrer, I'll make your life hell."

They bundled Nicholas into a car and drove off.

It was early evening at Ruzyne airport in Prague, when the Gestapo car pulled up with Hans and Nicholas. As Hans and the Gestapo Officers jumped out, they dragged Nicholas with them, out of the car and force—walked him into the building terminal.

Hans and the Gestapo Officers marched through the terminal, onto the tarmac of the Ruzyne airport. As dusk turned to night, the officers propelled Nicholas up the steps of the plane, almost about to take off.

Hans's face had a forbidding look, "Leave... and... don't... come... back."

His men shoved Nicholas inside the plane, as the hostess gaped in absolute terror.

"Shut the door!" shouted Hans.

The hostess pulled the door shut as Hans and his men strode down the steps.

Moments later the plane took off, with its engines roaring, almost relieved to be free of the soil of Prague.

Hans and his men stood on the side of the tarmac and observed as the plane disappeared into the horizon.

It was a late night in London when Nicholas eventually got home. He charged into his apartment in London and although his face was slightly bruised, he was fuming. When he took off his jacket, his Ma came in.

"Goodness me, what happened?" asked Barbara.

"Had an encounter with SS Officers," explained Nicholas.

"You should stay in London, son. Don't go back there," said Barbara.

"I'll go back if I have to. There is still a lot to do. The situation in Slovakia is getting worse than in Prague."

Chapter 20. Substandard Affairs in Prague

Night drew long shadows at the Lovosice Train Station in Prague, Northern Bohemia as David Belzer, in his mid—forties and his sons Adam, eleven, and Michael, twelve, waited for the train to arrive.

A station master, in his mid—forties, watched Belzer and his boys and as he spotted their yarmulkes, he headed towards them.

"You have to go inside there!" shouted the station master in German.

He pointed at the lavatory.

The boys looked at the sign above the waiting room: 'NO JEWS ALLOWED!'

"I insist!" shouted the station master.

He gestured towards the toilets.

The public men's room was dirty and cramped, with a lack of decent lighting. A room filled with urinals and filthy washbasins, with tarnished mixer tap and no place to spend more time in, than needed.

David, Adam and Michael entered. David walked to the sink and washed his face.

"Why are we here, dad?" asked Adam.

"We have to stay until the train arrives," said Belzer.

He finished cleaning his face.

"Remember when we were riding bicycles in the park?" asked Belzer.

Adam wandered around and stared at himself in the mirror as his eyes welled up. He turned to his father.

"What is the matter?" asked David.

"I want to stay here," said Adam.

"You'll have a much better life in England. Are you aware of what is happening here?" asked Belzer.

"Why can't you come with us, Dad?" asked Michael.

Belzer thought carefully.

"I am too old to start a new life in another country. It's going to be much better for you if you go," said David.

"I'm scared, Dad," said Adam.

"I promise. I'll send for you as soon as the situation here improves," said Belzer.

"What about school?" asked Michael.

"Schools are much better in England," promised Belzer.

"What about all of my friends here?" Michael continued.

"You'll make new friends," said Belzer.

"Dad, I…" began Adam, with tears in his eyes.

"I want you to be brave, son," said David.

He grabbed both of his sons and hugged them tightly, realizing this might be his last chance to do so, in his lifetime.

Suddenly, they heard as the train arrived at Lovosice train station. They stepped out of the men's restroom and made their way to the train.

David hugged Michael…and then Adam, one last time before they boarded the train.

"Look after your brother," said David.

"I will," promised Michael, and with those last words, Michael and Adam got on the train.

SS Officers were watching a family house in Prague.

Irma and Kareal Dvorak were there with their two daughters, Vera, who was seven and Eve, who was eleven. Irma got her daughter ready for school.

Suddenly Hans, Schulter and the other SS Officers approached the main door.

Hans nodded at the SS Officers and they commenced to smash their way in, barging into the house.

Irma looked terrified as she peered at the SS officers. Schulter strode up to her.

"What is this? What are you all…" began Irma in Czech.

Without a warning, Schulter slapped her hard. Instantly, she staggered back, almost falling.

"Speak German!" demanded Schulter in German.

Eve and Vera ran to their father, Kareal.

"We speak Czech in our household. German, only in your presence," admitted Kareal.

Schulter spat in Kareal's face. The saliva ran down Kareal's cheek.

Irma turned anxious. "We should all leave."

"I can't leave my business and have my life turned upside down. If I do, they…," began Kareal.

Schulter raised his hand once again.

The train arrived at the train station, one stop away from the border with Holland. The very moment the train stopped; Gestapo officers boarded it.

Inside of the train compartment, Josef, ten years old, sat worried, as he watched his brother Jakub who was only seven years old. Next to him was Anton, a mere six years old. He shied away, in fear, as his face turned red.

"Don't cry, Jakub. Everything will be fine!" comforted Josef.

The compartment door opened and the Gestapo Officers crowded in, as they checked it out. Another Gestapo officer waited outside.

Gestapo officers reached for Josef's suitcase and dumped its contents onto the floor, and then moved onto Jakub's suitcase.

Anton closed his eyes, as he shivered in fear.

"What is the matter with you?" Josef asked Anton in Czech.

Anton opened his eyes.

"I don't like them," said Anton.

The Gestapo officers eyed Anton, as he clutched his suitcase.

Anton glanced at the officer. "Don't touch it!"

The Gestapo officer placed his hand on Anton's shoulder.

"It's only a random check," assured the Gestapo officer in German.

Finally, after finishing, the Gestapo officer and his colleagues left and as the door shut, Anton and Jakob started to cry in earnest. Josef got up and went to sit between the two boys, hugging them and comforting them out of their fear.

Back in the heart of London, Nicholas stood in the reception room and grabbed the phone. He dialled a number off by heart, as Kate looked on.

"Tim? How is the situation over there? Hitler broke the terms of the Munich Agreement. Of course, he did. His actions should lead to more support for our efforts. I am going to find more foster families, more guarantors; Christians and Jews. We are doing everything possible. Is it? OK, stay safe. Speak soon," said Nicholas and with those words, hung up.

A huge steamboat was docked at the Hook of Holland. Children walked up the gangway, where an officer checked their passports. Everyone waited anxiously for whatever had to happen next. Some children looked curiously at their surroundings, while others were in tears, clearly overcome and still, others were bursting with excitement. As soon as their passports were checked and marked off on the passenger list, one after another, the children boarded the steamboat.

Hours later, the children gathered on the lower deck of a boat. An accordion somewhere struck up the national Czech anthem. The deck was filled with refugee children, with some happy to sing along, whilst others just sat and listened.

Chapter 21. Back In the Heart of England

Whilst the children continued on their voyage to England, at the Liverpool Street Station in London, families and visitors gathered, as they waited patiently for the train to arrive.

Further, along with the platform, Nicholas and uncle Shimon, in his mid—forties, with his yarmulke on his head, also stood waiting.

"It's already two hours late," said Nicholas.

"Normally, I wouldn't care about children but, under the circumstances, I feel obliged to help my family," said uncle Shimon.

"You did well. Goodness knows what would have happened to him if he had stayed," said Nicholas.

Uncle Shimon turned thoughtful. "Prague is unsafe for everyone now. What made you do it?"

"Do what?" asked Nicholas.

"To help. Why are you doing it?" asked uncle Shimon.

"I feel compelled to save them from an almost certain death."

"You're a mensch, only a few men would have the courage."

"Having ethics is a must. Every child deserves a chance. If I didn't step up, who knows what would happen?"

"What are you going to do when it is all over?" asked uncle Shimon.

Nicholas smiled, "I would love to do some fencing."

The train arrived in a cloud of steam.

Faces of children between the ages of three and fifteen years, filled the compartment windows, as they stared at the crowd of people. Kate and the other ladies, who held trays filled with food, were also waiting to feed hungry and thirsty 'tiny people'. Police officers watched attentively at the whole gathering and fuss.

The train stopped and Nicholas opened the doors to let the children off.

"This way, please. My name is Nicholas. Please, help yourself to a hot chocolate and a sandwich."

Rudolf approached and grabbed a sandwich off a lady's tray.

"You must be hungry," remarked Kate.

Rudolf nodded. Nicholas approached and read Rudolph's tag.

"What is your name?" asked Nicholas.

Rudolf smiled. "I am Rudolf."

"Of course, you are. Come with me. Your uncle is waiting for you," said Nicholas as he took Rudolf to uncle Shimon.

"Welcome to England, Rudolf," said uncle Shimon.

Rudolf hugged uncle Shimon, quite relieved that the journey had come to an end.

Maureen Adley and her husband, John, waited nervously as Kate came towards them.

"Can I check your ID's, please?" asked Kate.

"Yes, here they are…," said Maureen.

She showed her ID to Kate, as did John.

Kate crossed them off the clipboard.

"Wait here. It won't be long," said Kate.

Soon, Kate returned with a young girl.

"I recognize her. That is her…," said Maureen to John.

"This is the foster daughter you requested," announced Kate.

Maureen was overcome with relief as she hugged and kissed a young girl, with a mixture of tears and laughter.

"Welcome to England, my dear," said Maureen.

She hugged the young girl again.

"We are taking you to your new home," Maureen said.

The young girl was excited and thankful to be safe.

"Mr Adley. You are free to go. Please look after her," said Nicholas.

Rosie Williams and her husband Peter, in their mid—forties, focussed on Paulina, a wee little eight—year—old. Peter held a little Yorkshire Terrier.

"What a lovely girl," remarked Rosie.

Paulina smiled back but then became serious.

"I have a cup of tea and some biscuits ready for you at your new home," said Rosie.

Paulina appeared worried.

"Aren't you hungry?" asked Peter.

"Don't you want something to eat?" asked Rosie.

Paulina didn't respond.

"Do you want to go to the toilet?" asked Peter.

"My name is Paulina. What is your name?" asked Paulina in Czechoslovakian.

Rosie turned to her husband. "I don't understand what she's saying."

"My name is Paulina. What is your name?" asked Paulina in, German.

"Oh dear, I can't understand anything," said Rosie.

Peter gave the puppy to Paulina and hugged her.

"Come with us. We'll look after you," said Peter.

"I… am… hungry," mumbled Paulina in English.

"I can fix it. Here take this," said Rosie as she handed Paulina a sandwich.

Paulina looked up shyly and then opened the sandwich and took a huge bite, as she smiled.

As the morning came to a close, child after child left with their foster parents.

A female social worker, in her mid—forties, spotted Ada sitting on her suitcase.

"If her parents don't turn up, she'll have to come with me," the social worker said to Nicholas.

"That is fine," said Nicholas.

"What if her parents changed their minds? Will you be able to find a replacement family?" asked the social worker.

"I'll sort something out," said Nicholas.

As Ada started to cry, Nicholas rushed towards her with some biscuits. The social worker smiled.

"What is your name?" asked Nicholas.

"Ada," said the girl.

"Your family may not arrive until late this evening," said Nicholas.

Ada wiped her tears.

"Would you like some biscuits?" asked Nicholas, as Ada nodded.

"Here, have some."

He gave Ada a biscuit. She took a cautious bite and then smiled, as she ate it all.

"I want my sister with me," said Ada.

"Don't worry. I promise we will bring her over," said Nicholas.

"Will she stay with me?" asked Ada.

"I'll have a chat with your family. I'll make sure they take your sister in, too," said Nicholas.

Ada smiled and placed her arm forward. Nicholas chuckled as he gave her two more biscuits.

Chapter 22. A Hostile Situation in Prague

Tim looked out of the window and spotted the Gestapo as they marched down the street.

Occupied with paperwork, Doreen remained blissfully unaware, as she went through the documents and photographs of the children.

"They are everywhere. You need to leave the country," said Tim.

Tension suddenly rose in Doreen's office. As Tim stood at the window, he saw the black uniforms, as they ploughed their way through the street. Doreen joined him. Together, their eyes were fixed upon the source of their fear. They both knew this day would come and the inevitable had arrived.

"Where would I go?" asked Doreen.

"Poland would be safe," said Tim.

"You're right," said Doreen, resigned to her fate.

Worried, she packed her things in her bag.

"What about you?"

"I'll stay here until it's all over, and then I will leave," said Tim.

"Pray for me."

"Of course."

They hugged and with a sudden urgency, she left.

Doreen rushed out of the office, down an alley, desperate to get away to safety. Her very being was screaming danger. From around the corner, out of nowhere, Gestapo Officers appeared. Doreen froze and, in her heart, she realized that the moment she had feared, was upon her. A car stopped. Schulter and Hans stepped out and in seconds, dragged Doreen inside. Within a minute, Doreen and the car were gone and the rest of the Gestapo disappeared into thin air, with none the wiser.

Hans held Doreen tight and she could feel his tepid breath on her neck. He grabbed her hair, lifting her face to Shulter. Hands were everywhere, as they touched and felt, spaces on her skin, she had not permitted. She felt sick to her stomach and yet oddly detached. Her legs were forced and her arms held back, aggression in every touch, every smear, bruising her softest flesh, tearing her most delicate skin. Her stockings were shredded and tatters of silk fabric hung around her feet. And then, as if aroused from a stupor, she fought back, catching Shulter on the cheek with her elbow. His head snapped back and she could see the madness in his eyes. Shulter swung back his arm and she saw as his fist came for her face. His fist connected and pain exploded in her head, with blood that spurted from her nose. She hardly had time to recover when she felt the next blow to her eye, and immediately felt it begin to swell. The next blow fell on the side of her cheek and she felt darkness start to descend, just before the blows rained down on her in quick succession.

"Where were you going? Wake up…WAKE UP! I want you awake for this." shouted Schulter.

He tore at her blouse, bruising and battering her sensitive feminity.

"You Deutsche pig!" screamed Doreen.

Her arm snacked free and she tore into Schulter with all her might.

"What are you working on?" asked Schulter as he slapped her across her chest.

The fight intensified and Schulter pummelled her face again.

"Get your hands off me!" Doreen screamed hysterically as she struggled to protect herself, kicking, butting and hitting hard.

"Let this be a lesson Frau Warner, mind your own business!" said Schulter.

Suddenly Hans opened the door and Schulter threw Doreen out of the vehicle.

Doreen crashed onto the street, totally disoriented as her head hit the concrete. Blood poured down her face and she staggered to her feet. Anger, shame, humiliation coursed through her veins as she tried to piece together her blouse and pick up the tatters of her clothing around her feet. Mortified, she looked around her, but she was alone and although her head spun, she forced herself to start walking as fast as she could. Every cell in her body pulsed her to flee for her life, aware that her very existence was in grave danger but unaware that Hans shadowed her every move.

Chapter 23. In Constant Need of More Foster Parents

An early evening in London and it was just after six when Nicholas sat down behind his desk in his London apartment. Jonathan and Barbara Smith and their daughter Chloe still stood, as Kate hovered nearby, regarding the girl that held onto her mother's leg.

"I am glad you came. Things are getting worse," said Nicholas.

Nicholas showed them the catalogue. Jonathan took it and went through the catalogue slowly. He stopped at a photo and bent down to show the picture to Chloe.

"Those two girls are nice," said Jonathan.

Nicholas looked at the picture. Evka and Janka were cute, despite their grave faces.

"That's Evka Jahoda, she is seven years old. And this is her sister, Janka. She is six years old," said Nicholas.

"They could be your older sisters," said Jonathan to Chloe.

Barbara turned to Chloe. "Do you like them?"

Chloe hesitated, then hugged Barbara and shied away.

Nicholas went through the hallway as he walked Jonathan, Barbara and Chloe to the front door.

"We'll do our best to make them feel comfortable," promised Barbara.

"They will be in good hands, I am sure," said Nicholas.

Jonathan, Barbara, and Chloe departed.

Nicholas shut the door and turned back to make his way to his office.

Nicholas walked back to the reception room wearily and sat down in his armchair.

Kate leant against the desk and noticed the toll that finding homes for the children, had taken on Nicholas.

"Such a lovely family. You did well there."

"I hope everything works out fine," he said, as the front doorbell rang.

"It looks like they have forgotten something," said Nicholas.

"I will get that," said Kate, as she walked towards the door.

As she opened the front door, two rabbis, Aharon and Natan, in their mid—thirties, stood on the door-step.

"How may I help?" asked Kate.

"We want an explanation!" demanded Aharon rudely.

"A what...?" said Kate.

Nicholas turned up after hearing the angry voices.

"Gentlemen, how can I help?" asked Nicholas.

"What you are doing to Jewish families is wrong," said Aharon.

"You have split siblings, torn families apart, placed Jewish children in Christian households. That's not God's way," insisted Natan.

"Well, the alternative is..."

"You must stop! It's against our beliefs," said Aharon.

"With all respect, I care about those children. A Jewish child raised by a Christian family is much better off than a dead one," said Nicholas.

"Jewish children must not grow up in Christian homes," said Aharon.

"It's against the Torah," added Natan.

The unwelcome visit was quickly getting out of hand, with the rabbi's angered, beyond logic. Nicholas gave them a stern, forbidding look and possessed of patience, he did not know he had, he said, "Gentlemen, thank you for your visit. Goodnight."

Nicholas shut the door on the rabbis.

Moments later, Nicholas peeked from behind curtains and made sure no one was outside. As the rabbis moved down the road, he spotted a black car parked across the road, with three men that sat inside.

Nicholas appeared puzzled and affronted.

"What a disgrace. Is following the Torah, more important than the welfare of the children? If they want the children to stay with Jewish families, then give me Jewish foster parents. I just want the children safe."

"They don't have a clue what those children are going through," agreed Kate.

"Have you seen anything out of the ordinary?" asked Nicholas.

"Like what?" asked Kate.

Nicholas looked out of the window again.

"That car across the road. It's been there for several hours," said Nicholas.

"Really?" asked Kate.

"You should stay here tonight. It may not be safe for you to go home, you can have the room next to Ma," worried Nicholas.

"If you say so…," said Kate.

Nicholas pulled the curtains shut, with a finality.

At the desk in Doreen's office, Tim browsed through some papers. He looked up at the door as he heard shuffling in the hallway.

Suddenly, Doreen dragged herself in, hardly able to stand and so pummelled, that she started to cough up blood.

Tim leapt to his feet and rushed towards her.

"Doreen…Doreen…no…just look at you…what happened!?" asked Tim.

"Gestapo," muttered Doreen thickly through her swollen lips, before she fainted in his arms.

Tim grabbed her before she hit the floor and lay her down gently.

He rushed over to the desk and grabbed the bottle of water. Pulling his scarf from his neck, he wet the side of the scarf and started to wipe the blood off Doreen's face. Everything in him had gone cold, he knew they were in peril.

Suddenly that door crashed open and Hans and Schulter stepped in, with malevolent grins on their faces. Sweat broke out on Tim's forehead.

Chapter 24. Asking for Support

While the situation in Prague seemed to get more complicated by the minute, in London, Nicholas and Kate were frantically sorting out documents. Families all over London had offered to foster children, but time was running out and they could feel the window of opportunity slowly starting to close.

"I'm overwhelmed. All this support from all those families. That's so kind of them," said Kate.

"Looking after someone else's child isn't easy," said Nicholas.

The phone on the desk rang and Kate picked it up.

"How may I help?" asked Kate.

Kate's face blanched and she handed the phone to Nicholas.

"Tim?! What?! That's outrageous! Is she okay? Yes, please," said Nicholas.

Nicholas rubbed his face, tense and shocked at the events in Prague.

"We are putting ourselves at risk for these children. Yes, I am listening. Again?! How much this time? A hundred missing? How? Who? A thousand for the train to leave the station? By when?"

A beat went by.

"Yes. I'll try to get it by noon tomorrow. Take care."

Nicholas hung up and turned to Kate. "They have captured Doreen... and money is missing."

"What?" asked Kate, shocked.

"I have to speak to Bob," said Nicholas.

The next afternoon, Nicholas headed to the Fencing Club in London.

He entered the room filled with fencing gloves, masks and cups on the shelves on the walls. An excitement infused the air as the club was overflowing with several of the members of the fencing club. Searching for Bob, he found him and his friends gathered around a table. Bob was engaged in an animated conversation with a club member, about the pros and cons of the Passata Soto. Nicholas was just about to walk across to them when Bob recognized him and waved him over.

"Nicholas, what brings you here? I thought you were busy," said Bob.

"I am, but.... we need to talk," said Nicholas.

"What about, Nicholas?" asked Bob, surprise written on his face.

"I have little time old chap. I like to have a word with you if you please?" asked Nicholas, lifting his eyebrows at the surrounding friends.

Bob looked around as he grimaced.

"Well, I am comfortable here. What is that you want?"

"Listen, Bob, I need a favour from you. I need to borrow a thousand pounds. It's to pay for the children's transport," said Nicholas.

"A thousand pounds!?" said Bob, shocked.

"I know. I'll make it back and pay it in full," promised Nicholas.

"I would prefer to invest money in property," said Bob. "There is no guarantee I will get my money back. It's a risky business and not a profitable one."

"Look, you know I am good for it. And for goodness sake, a child's life is more important than a house. And Bob… I need to fly to Prague for a few days," said Nicholas.

"Again? You better move and find a job there. You will run out of money soon," warned Bob.

"I need to finish what I've started."

"Don't! It will be the ruin of you chum. Let the problems stay on that side of the ocean, we are all having a good time here," said Bob.

Nicholas was out of time and out of patience.

"I need the money now. I'll pay it back as soon as I am done with my work," said Nicholas.

Bob stood up, having made up his mind.

"Very well, come along then," said Bob.

Kate sat at the desk and completed the forms. She heard Nicholas enter the apartment and stood up, just as he came into the study, agitated and frustrated.

"I've got the money," said Nicholas.

"That's great," she smiled at him, trying to lighten his mood.

Nicholas's face became concerned.

"I'll have to fly to Prague. I can't let things go wrong there. The lives of a lot of children are at stake."

"Of course, Nicholas."

Nicholas picked up the phone and dialled.

"Hello, Tim. We'll have to reschedule the evacuation for the thirtieth of August. Yeah, I've sorted out the money. I'll be arriving tonight. See you then," said Nicholas before he hung up the telephone.

Chapter 25. Knocking at the Door of the Gestapo Headquarters

It was an early evening at the Ruzyne airport in Prague. Nicholas came out from the terminal and headed for a cab.

"Gestapo Headquarters please," said Nicholas to the driver, who took one look at Nicholas's face and realized that his fare meant serious business.

The driver shuddered and quickly headed off.

The cab pulled up in front of the local Gestapo headquarters.

"Wait here," he asked the cab driver.

Nicholas stepped out and walked directly up to the two Gestapo officers, that stood with their machine guns, at the door.

"I want to speak with the commander! I insist on the immediate release of Mrs Doreen Warner!" demanded Nicholas.

The Gestapo officers conversed between themselves. One officer went into the building, and he shouted in German.

Nicholas waited, his face resolute, brooking no argument, impatient and on edge.

Hans sauntered out, with a silly grin on his face.

"What do you want?" asked Hans.

"I am here to save your bacon, Hans. It's about Mrs Doreen Warner. Release her immediately," said Nicholas.

"What?! My bacon you say. Why should I listen to you?" mocked Hans, as he burst out laughing.

Nicholas waited unperturbed until Hans's tirade was finished.

With deadly calm, he continued. "Mrs Warner is being held illegally and against her will. She works for the British government old' chap."

Hans's expression changed from thinking he held the upper hand, to knowing he was the underdog in seconds.

"What if I don't release her?" asked Hans.

"Tut, tut, tut…. You know how this will go. I'll treat this as a diplomatic incident and inform the British government," stated Nicholas.

"You're bluffing."

"Am I Hans? Am I? You might be surprised to know how just how well—connected I am with both the British and your German government. I would not overplay my hand if I were you," said Nicholas.

Hans blanched as he saw the truth of the determination in Nicholas's eyes. He quickly turned around and went back inside.

Nicholas waited, standing ramrod, ready to storm the barracks if need until the door opened. Hans pushed Doreen out, weak and bruised, she crashed to the ground and Nicholas rushed to her aid.

"Doreen, little one, are you all, right?" asked Nicholas.

"I am fine," the words came through swollen and bloodied lips. Her eyes were almost swollen shut, purple bruising all over her face. Doreen showed her mettle and fought, and won the battle to stand up.

"I am glad you came," she whispered. Nicholas looked into her eyes and saw the depth of the depravity that she had endured. The violence took hold of him.

Nicholas glared at Hans and he made Hans an unsaid promise, he intended to keep.

He put his arm around Doreen's shoulder and helped her limp from the waiting cab.

At Doreen's office, on a desk laden with passports, Dalek sat and prepared the children's passports. Nicholas walked in with a stronger but still limping Doreen.

"How are things here?" asked Nicholas.

"Passports are ready...," said Dalek, shocked to the core, as he stared at the damage on Doreen's face, that his collaboration had caused. Ashamed in himself, Dalek let his head down and refused to look at Doreen again. Doreen walked over to the bathroom and closed the door. The silence between Nicholas and Dalek was deafening. Nicholas kept staring at Dalek and Dalek refused to look up.

When Doreen came out, her face was cleaned and she had applied some foundation and lipstick. She had changed her clothes and shoes and tidied her hair. She looked up at Nicholas and he read a steel determination, that belied what her body said.

Doreen took the passports and put them in her bag, as she headed slowly for the door. Nicholas watched her in admiration. A lesser woman would have run for the hills, but despite the immense trauma and pain she had experienced the last two days, she was back in the fight!

"Have you arranged for more money?" asked Dalek.

"I have," confirmed Nicholas.

"It's on my way home. I can pay it today," said Dalek.

"Don't worry. I'll sort it all out tomorrow morning," said Nicholas.

Annoyed and afraid, Dalek put on his jacket and walked out.

Chapter 26. Increasing Rigidity at the Wilson Train Station

The door of Mr Cibulka's house in Sudetenland, Prague, opened and Dominik Cibulka rushed towards the bedroom and headlong towards the bed. He awoke his daughter, Kristina.

"Sweetheart. We need to go," said Dominik in Czech.

"Daddy…"

"We need to go now!" insisted Dominik, his words tainted by fear.

He pulled Kristina from the bed and wrapped her in a crispy blanket. He ran out as he cradled his daughter. He raced down the dark alleyway. Kristina cried out and the Gestapo spotted him.

"Stop! Stop!" shouted the Gestapo.

Dominik ignored them.

The Gestapo officers reacted swiftly and with anger and they opened fire.

Dominik and Kristina were stroked with bullets and they collapsed almost instantly. Covered in blood and paralyzed by slivers of pain, their worlds both turned dark within seconds.

Whilst the last breath left Dominik, and Kristina's heart beat its last refrain, families and children were gathered on the Wilson Train Station platform, as they apprehensively waited for the train to arrive. Paper tags hung off the children's necks.

Doreen read the names on children's tags and crossed their names off the clipboard.

"Helene Bondyova. Bohdan Matusek. Kristina Cibulka."

No answer.

"Kristina Cibulka?" Doreen read out.

Once again, no response.

She looked at Kristina's tag and recognition dawned on her. Kristina was missing and the Gestapo had something to do with it.

Her horror was evident on her face and as the parents saw it, a frenetic urgency settled over parents and children alike and escalated as the minutes passed. In the midst of, the almost panic, Nicholas appeared.

"Where is Tim?" asked Nicholas.

"He is not here. Neither is Kristina Cibulka," said Doreen.

"She should be here already. She'll miss the train," worried Nicholas.

"She is not coming to Nicholas, I just know it. This is the Gestapo's doing," Doreen whispered softly but sadly to Nicholas.

Nicholas and Doreen both shuddered with the thoughts of what could have happened to Tim.

Tim collected the last papers and headed out of Doreen's office. Soon after he landed on the street, he spotted the Gestapo officers. Giving up all pretence, he turned around and fled in the other direction.

The Gestapo officers chased after him and eventually caught up with him. They slapped Tim around, then hauled Tim off his feet and marched over to a van standing by the curb, throwing him inside head—first.

Doreen looked at her watch and then stared at the gate to the Wilson train station. Nicholas looked worried, contemplating just how long he could still wait.

"Tim, where are you?" muttered Doreen to herself.

"We have to act now. I have a feeling something dreadful has happened," said Nicholas.

Nicholas ran to the side of the platform and started to move luggage onto the train, urgently helping parents board their children, as quickly as possible, onto the train.

"Have a safe trip!" Nicholas said as he moved on to the next family.

A mother in her mid—thirties approached Nicholas.

"Thank you, good man," said the woman.

"You're welcome, ma'am. Please would you excuse me, I have quite a few families that still require my assistance," said Nicholas.

Nicholas hurried over and lifted more children onto the train, whilst pushing their luggage through the windows, frantic to get the train moving.

Chapter 27. Dicey Condition at the Gestapo Headquarters

Dalek sat on a chair at the Gestapo Headquarters, severely beaten up, with blood oozing from his ear and the many cuts on his face, half—conscious with his head sideways.

Hans, Schulter and a few other Gestapo officers gazed at him and spoke in German behind his back.

"The water tank is ready," said Hans.

Schulter turned to Dalek.

"Where are Doreen Warner and the Englishman?" asked Schulter.

Head down, Dalek mumbled some words, as he tried to balance his need to redeem his shame, with that of preserving his life.

"Speak up!" demanded Schulter.

Hans and the Gestapo officer dragged Dalek to the tank that was filled with iced water.

"You don't want to talk?" asked Schulter.

A deathly silence filled the room and Dalek could hear every irregular beat of his fluttered, fearful heart. Schulter forced Dalek onto his knees.

"Maybe this will make you talk," said Schulter.

The Gestapo officer pushed Dalek's head into the water.

Dalek flailed and slammed his hand against the tank in sheer desperation.

Schulter and Gestapo Officer held Dalek underwater for a few seconds more and then pulled him out. Dalek came out of the water, pale and heaving for air, as he coughed out the water that had filled his throat and nose.

"Are you ready to talk?" asked Schulter.

No response came from Dalek as he started to struggle against Hans.

"Again!" demanded Schulter.

He shoved Dalek hard and kept him underwater for a lot longer, as he waited until he saw Dalek's struggles start to lessen, as his strength waned. He yanked Dalek out and threw him on the floor.

Dalek flailed on the floor, as he threw his arms and legs in the air and convulsed, as his lungs tried to rid themselves of the drowning water. He wheezed, spluttered and gasped desperately for air, as he clawed at his throat. A fire burned in his nasal cavities and deep in his throat.

"Where is she?" asked Schulter.

The Gestapo officer lifted Dalek onto his knees and then hit him in the face with all his strength. Dalek's head snapped back and he fell to the floor in agony.

Dalek screamed and made squirming movements, every part of his body throbbing with pain.

Two Gestapo officers dragged a badly bruised and battered Dalek to his feet. They held him up, as he could barely stand.

Schulter took out his gun and pointed it at Dalek's head.

"This is your last chance. Where is Doreen Warner?" asked Schulter.

"She is helping children get out of the country," mumbled Dalek, in utter defeat, as he started to whimper in pain.

Schulter trained his gun on Dalek.

"Who is behind this?" asked Schulter.

Dalek stayed quiet, almost too far gone to answer.

"Warner! Where is she!?" yelled Hans.

"She helps the Englishman get children out of the country," said Dalek.

"Where are they!?"

Dalek kept silent, as he hung onto his sanity and dignity by a thread.

"You better talk if you want your wife and your baby to stay alive," said Hans.

Dalek felt torn, but not willing to sacrifice his family, he spoke.

"At the train station!" mumbled Dalek, as tears coursed down his cheeks, ashamed at his betrayal.

The Gestapo officers threw Dalek onto the floor and left in a hurry for the station.

Chapter 28. The Train Blowing the Whistle

At the Wilson train station, Antonin Jahoda, in his mid—thirties, set a suitcase down on the luggage wagon. He hoisted his daughters, Evka and Janka, on board.

Antonin opened the door and put his daughters' suitcase in the luggage hold.

He hugged Evka and Janka tightly, the emotion almost choking him. The girls were heartbroken and instinctively realized that this goodbye was different, almost as if this was the last time, they would see or touch their dad.

"You will be all right. England is a nice place," said Doreen.

Antonin nodded at Doreen and looked back at his daughters.

"Repeat after me…I am hungry!" said Antonin.

"I… am… hungry, " said Evka.

"I… am… hungry," said Janka.

"I need a toilet," said Antonin.

"I… need… toilet," said Evka.

The train whistle blew and the moment was upon them. Antonin hugged and kissed his precious Evka and Janka for the last time. Standing on the platform, he watched them as they peeked from the open window. Antonin grabbed Janka's and Evka's hands through the window.

"My daughters. You'll be fine," said Antonin.

Evka cried out, whilst Janka clutched his hand, not wanting to let go. Antonin wrenched his hand free and stood dejected, as he waved to his daughters, while they passed from his sight.

The last steam from the train engulfed Antonin as the train slowly left the station.

Nicholas smiled to himself as the train disappeared down the tracks.

As he turned back to the platform, he spotted the Gestapo officers, as they streamed into the other side of the station.

"Too late, chaps. You'll never win," said Nicholas confidently and with a jaunt in his step, he turned around and left the station.

References:

Books:

Mináč, M., *The Lottery of Life, Prague, W.I.P. sro., 2007.*

Muriel, M & Gissing V., *Nicholas Winton and the Rescued Generation*, London, Vallentine Mitchell, 2001.

Warriner, H., *Doreen Warriner's War*, Leicestershire, The Book Guild Ltd., 2019.

Winton, B., *If it's Not Impossible… The Life of Sir Nicholas Winton*, Leicestershire, Matador, 2014.

Internet sources:

McFadden, R.D., *Nicholas Winton, Rescuer of 669 Children from Holocaust, Dies at 106.,* The New York Times, www.nytimes.com

United States Holocaust Memorial Museum, *Nicholas Winton and The Rescue of Children from Czechoslovakia, 1938 – 1939,* United States Holocaust Memorial Museum, Washington, DC, Nicholas Winton and the Rescue of Children from Czechoslovakia, 193… | Holocaust Encyclopedia (ushmm.org)

BBC, *WW2: How did one Englishman save 669 children from the Holocaust?* WW2: How did one Englishman save 669 children from the Holocaust? — BBC Teach

Holocaust Day Memorial Trust, *Sir Nicholas Winton,* Holocaust Memorial Day Trust | Sir Nicholas Winton (hmd.org.uk)

The National Holocaust Centre and Museum, *Nicholas Winton*, Holocaust Memorial Day Trust | Sir Nicholas Winton (hmd.org.uk)

YouTube:

Children Saved from the Nazis: The Story of Sir Nicholas Winton, YouTube, www.youtube.com/watch?v=n-ToyPjjoUqQ&t=1894s

Sir Nicholas Winton, November 2014 – BBC HARDtalk, YouTube, www.youtube.com/watch?v=NO63ajFFh-Do&t=55s

60 Minutes: Sir Nicholas Winton "Saving the Children", YouTube, www.youtube.com/watch?v=coaoifN-ziKQ&t=368s

Miscellaneous:

Nicholas Winton: The Power of Good (DVD), Executive Producer — Martina Štolbová, Produced by: Matej Mináč and Patrik Pašš, 2002.